She'd reacted badly to Sylvia's secret. What if Sylvia wouldn't forgive her?

Crystal tapped gently on the door, fighting the urge to scurry away. Sylvia would yell at her. Crystal should give her that chance. She deserved a sound scolding. It would loosen up the knot of guilt forming in her belly. Sylvia's wrath would ease the wave of self-hatred washing over her. Everyone would feel better after.

Crystal practiced her apology. She played out in her mind what Sylvia might say and what her answers might be. In reality, Crystal would probably just sit there and let Sylvia scream at her. It was foolish to presume she'd defend her actions. Sylvia hated excuses. Then again, she was well versed in Crystal's panic attacks.

It was possible she would be more annoyed than angry. If they let the sun go down on an argument, it might disenchant Sylvia with their date. It had to be now. Crystal couldn't take that chance.

The doorknob circled callously in her hand. It gave no notice of the horrible scene awaiting Crystal's arrival. She stepped into the apartment. It was dark. Crystal expected it to be a mess. Sylvia threw things when she was upset. She knocked things over. Everything was as Crystal had left it. The apartment was wrapped in stillness.

She lost her voice. She didn't remember screaming, but her voice was hoarse for three days after.

They each have a secret that could destroy their relationship...

Crystal and Sylvia are best friends, each the only one the other one trusts. But they each have a dark secret, and neither one knows how to tell the other. Crystal's secret is that she's gay and strongly attracted to Sylvia. She wants more than friendship, but she's afraid to destroy what they already have by letting Sylvia know. And after all, friendship is better than nothing, isn't it? But Sylvia's secret is more sinister. It could not only destroy their friendship, it could also hurt Crystal—in more ways than one.

KUDOS for *A Turbulent Affair*

In *A Turbulent Affair* by Sarah Doebereiner, Crystal is in love with her best friend Sylvia, but she's afraid to let her know because Sylvia doesn't know that Crystal is into girls, and Crystal's afraid that telling Sylvia how she feels will destroy their relationship. On the other hand, Sylvia can't maintain a relationship with anyone but Crystal, and every man she dates abandons her when he finds out her secret obsession. Sylvia's afraid that Crystal will do the same. Needless to say, the relationship between these two young women is complicated with both of them afraid to trust enough to confess their secrets. To be honest, this genre makes me a bit uncomfortable, but the author handled it with skill and an amazing depth of understanding of what it was like for both women—for Crystal, who has never had a lover, as well as for Sylvia, who doesn't really like men, but who never considered any other options. The story is told with skill, subtlety, and sensitivity. ~ *Taylor Jones, Reviewer*

A Turbulent Affair by Sarah Doebereiner is the story of two young women, Crystal and Sylvia. Crystal is gay and in love with Sylvia, who is *not*—at least as far as she knows. Crystal's hesitant to tell Sylvia her secret for fear that Sylvia will break off their friendship. But Sylvia also has a secret that she is afraid to confess to Crystal for the very same reason. The result is a complicated, heart-breaking, heart-warming, and sometimes tragic story of love, need, obsession, distrust, and fear where two women turn to each other when they can't make it work with anyone else. Doebereiner did an excellent job of describing both the sweetness of the romance and the situational awkwardness of forging your way into unknown territory, both for Crystal who has never had sex, or even a romantic relationship, as well as for Sylvia who has never thought of women in "that way" before and really isn't certain of her own sexual orientation. *A Turbulent Affair* is, by its very nature, a difficult story to tell and the author's understanding of both sides of the issues comes across in the sensitivity and compassion with which she tells it. Whatever your sexual orientation, you can't help but root for both troubled women as they struggle to accept each other unconditionally, despite their flaws and quirks, while taking their relationship to a different, and difficult, level, without destroying their precious friendship. It gives you a new appreciation for how hard life can sometimes be for some people. ~ *Regan Murphy, Reviewer*

ACKNOWLEDGEMENTS

Special thanks to the Black Opal Books team for all of the hard work and dedication that went into making this book a reality

A
Turbulent
Affair

Sarah Doebereiner

A Black Opal Books Publication

Black Opal Books

BECAUSE SOME STORIES JUST HAVE TO BE TOLD

GENRE: ROMANCE F/F/NEW ADULT/ROMANTIC SUSPENSE

A TURBULENT AFFAIR
Copyright © 2016 by Sarah Doebereiner
Cover Design by Jackson Cover Designs
All cover art copyright © 2016
All Rights Reserved
Print ISBN: 978-1-626943-99-5

First Publication: JANUARY 2016

Published by Black Opal Books **http://www.blackopalbooks.com**

DEDICATION

*For the people who love me as I am
and never try to make me less.*

Chapter 1

INTRODUCTIONS

Crystal hovered around her kitchen. She opened the refrigerator door to see how many cans of soda were inside. Her slender shadow stretched across the floor. The light bulb in the kitchen hung down far enough to brim over the edge of the fixture. It was brighter than it should have been. An abrasive glow made the room look dirty. Every shadow turned into grime, even though she'd scrubbed the floor that morning.

She peered into the living room. It was comfortably lit. Everything in it was simple and functional. There was a floor lamp behind the couch. Neither the couch nor the lamp matched the colors of the carpet or wallpaper. If pressed to describe it, Crystal always tried to use words like minimalistic, rather than poor. Her television sat on a cardboard box. *Crys's junk* was written on the box in large, black sharpie. It was a woman's writing, but not Crystal's. It was big, sloppy, and ostentatious.

Another box filled the space in front of the couch where a coffee table would have gone. This box was scuffed on one side from having feet pressed against it. There were rings on the top of the box from condensation. Multiple rings were present, but they were clustered together in two tight patterns. Crystal smiled to herself. Two people sat on that couch. Two people rested drinks on the box-table. Two cups placed over and over in the same two spots, until the box had started to be eaten away by the drips they shed.

Crystal turned back to the kitchen and swung open a cupboard door. She glanced inside at the perfect stacks of cups and bowls. For a moment, she was transfixed by her own scrawny reflection in the glass. She slicked down a few tiny hairs standing at attention in the thick of her left eyebrow. The shirt she was wearing billowed around her. It swallowed her curves alive, but the hue brought out flecks of green in her eyes. The hem of the sleeves fell past her hands. She shook her head lightly and crossed to the refrigerator.

Eight cans of soda nested on the shelf. But the one closest to her was already opened—seven cans of soda, she corrected herself. When she picked up the eighth can, she could still hear the fizz crackling inside. *Fresh enough for me.*

The can made her sleeve feel cold. It camouflaged the sweat that was settling in her palm. She passed the soda from one hand to the other and let the chill sink into her. Then she rubbed the fabric of her sleeve against her palm. The tips of her fingers wiped away lingering moisture.

Crystal sucked in air until her organs felt cramped by the fullness of her lungs. She walked into the living room, sat on the couch, and pulled her feet up to chest. Her blue jeans bunched at the knee and hip where her slender limbs bent.

Several times she brought the can of soda to her lips. The motion was too shallow to pull liquid into her mouth. The third mock sip splashed the skin just under her nose. She used her sleeve to wipe her face. When she realized what she had done, she rubbed the sleeve against the coarse fabric of the couch. Fatter fibers in the linens soaked up sticky soda.

Company was coming. The couch was damp. She wiped the spot with the same sleeve. Her feet wouldn't settle. First, they landed in her smudges on the box. Then they felt better flat on the floor. Crossed, uncrossed, shaking gently. They were getting too worked up. They were their own entity, full of nervous energy that she couldn't control. She set the can in her box ring and ran a hand through hair. Chestnut brown flyaways jumped out from their sculpting. Her cell phone flashed seven o'clock.

Across the room, someone jostled the door. It rattled on its hinges, but didn't give. The tension in Crystal's body spring-boarded her to a standing position. Before she could reach the door, knocking reverberated in the entry way. The visitor jiggled the handle more forcefully.

"Crys?" Sylvia's voice drifted in like a melody—an annoyed melody. Crystal hesitated. She didn't want to open the door too quickly and look like she was waiting. The motion was a dance. She took a few steps: backward, forward, backward. Where was the line between casual and rude?

"Coming," she answered. After what seemed like long enough, she meandered to the door and unlocked it.

Sylvia thrust the door open forcefully as soon as the deadbolt clicked. It slammed into the tip of Crystal's foot before she could step back. The first three toes throbbed. She held a yelp behind clenched teeth. Crystal waited for Sylvia to walk in the room first. It would be less noticeable if she happened to limp on the first step. Crystal crossed one arm over her chest and peered into the front yard.

"Just you?" she mused, before she closed the door.

Sylvia plopped down on the couch. She shot Crystal a flat smile. It was a pinched, thin line under her nose that fell short of her eyes.

Strands of silky, black hair fell down around her face, shadowing her jaw line. Her lips were painted with gloss. She puffed them into a pout. A few loose strands of hair stuck in the gloss. "Why'd you lock it?" she asked.

Her tone was hard to read. Crystal unrolled the hem of her shirt. She frowned and glanced from the door to Sylvia. Her lips felt suddenly dry. They stuck together when she opened them to speak. She twisted her tongue sideways over bottom lip.

"Did you leave Jason in the car?" she asked.

She wiggled her toes in her socks and wondered if Sylvia was ashamed of her. The thought made her throat tighten. Crystal tried to breathe deeply, but her mouth watered. She swallowed her nerves. The thick, slimy spit made her stomach ache. Sylvia was no longer smiling. She rubbed her face like she was trying to wipe her own frown away.

"Oh," Crystal added.

The look on Sylvia's face made everything clear to Crystal. It was a face she had seen before. Jason didn't show. It looked worse than just a broken date. Crystal felt her arms sinking down to her sides. Her neck was stiff from holding her shoulders up. Jason didn't come. More than that, it was probably over between them. Crystal leapt onto couch. She landed half-way on top of Sylvia before rolling into her side.

"You smashed my foot when you opened the door," Crystal confessed. She nudged Sylvia's body with her shoulder. "I think it's broken."

She collapsed into the fetal position and waved her

foot in Sylvia's face. Their laughter loosened up the air in the apartment. It reverberated in every corner, until Crystal felt at home again.

Then there was silence. Crystal watched Sylvia stare at the black screen of the television. Solidarity wafted between them. For Crystal, it was a comfortable silence. Sylvia always went at her own pace.

Crystal stretched to pick up her can of soda, but couldn't shift her focus from Sylvia. She "under reached" and hit the can with the tip of her fingers. It wobbled, but didn't fall over. Sylvia looked at her. Crystal pulled her empty hand back and tucked it in-between her knees. The tips of her fingers sucked in heat from her legs.

"Klutz much?" Sylvia said.

Crystal studied the lines in Sylvia's face and laughed anyway. She always laughed at Sylvia's jokes, even when she wasn't in a position to be joking. Maybe, especially, when it was inappropriate. That's when Sylvia needed a laugh from her most.

Sylvia was a stoic sort of person. She was passionate, but guarded much of the time. For some reason, she couldn't keep her feelings in check when she looked at Crystal. Crystal had a "yes face." There was a kindness in her eyes that split open Sylvia's belly and let her guts come rushing out. There was no use fighting it.

"I don't know what happened," she admitted.

"Want to talk about it?"

The two were sitting close together. They were

touching from the shoulder to the hips, but there was a gap between their legs. Crystal's knees were angled toward Sylvia. Both of their arms were at their sides. The contact was passive, coincidental.

"Not on an empty stomach," Sylvia replied.

"You're in luck. I went to the store to stock up since you two..." Crystal trailed off. It wasn't a meet the boyfriend night. She bit the side of her cheek. "Since I just got paid and all I had was half-sour milk and the gross Chinese you left the other day." She stood and glided into the kitchen to pop popcorn. It was their favorite snack for break ups. It was packed with delicious, buttery I-don't-care-how-fat-I-get taste without many guilt-inspiring calories.

Sylvia sipped Crystal's soda. "Why can't I just find someone...I don't know...*perfect*?" She over-accentuated the word perfect. Her mouth wrapped around it as though it was a foreign concept, like she had never said the word before.

"You always go for the wrong kind of guy," Crystal answered.

Crystal's words were clearly audible, but Sylvia pretended not to notice. She replaced the can of soda to its ring and wandered into the kitchen.

Crystal's kitchen was cramped. She had a round table squished into the corner. It was oblong. A square one would have fit better. It sat four, but she only had two chairs. One of them wobbled unbearably. Sylvia pulled it out, moved it aside, and sat on top of the table. There was a small bag on the table beside her. She scooted it behind her to avoid sitting on it. Crystal opened the refrigerator door. She smiled at seven sodas in the fridge. A picture of Sylvia and Crystal hung on the freezer door. Crystal didn't have any magnets, so she had covered it in clear tape to keep it stuck in place and clean. In the picture, Crystal's head was leaning on Sylvia's shoulder.

The pose lent a hunch to Crystal's shoulders. She was already petite. In the picture, she was folded in on herself like a paper doll. The picture was taken at a carnival, in front of the balloon dart game. The little pops made Crystal turn into Sylvia's hair, so her face was partially obscured. It was Crystal's favorite picture. Sylvia had both hands in front of her. She tossed up a double peace sign at the last moment. Her mouth was open and her tongue was out. Crystal smiled gently. That was a good day.

"What did you say? Your microwave sounds like it's from the 1940s," Sylvia said between chuckles.

"You always end up with guys who don't realize how awesome you are," Crystal stated.

Her tone was cautious. Sylvia hated compliments. Crystal ducked inside the open fridge. It served as a buffer between them. Having that barrier gave her the courage to repeat herself a little louder. She closed the door and handed Sylvia a fresh can of soda. Crystal's heart fluttered in her chest. It was difficult for her to speak frankly, even with Sylvia. The pounding in her chest radiated down her arms. She leaned against the counter in case her heart jumped into her head and made her dizzy.

"I really thought it was going well this time." Sylvia voiced her disappointment through a sigh. She opened the soda and wiggled the pop top until it came loose in her hand. She pushed it inside the can. Crystal worried she might choke on it when she took the last sip. It made her crazy, but she didn't say it. "We were interested in the same things," Sylvia continued. "He liked spinach Alfredo pizza. I mean who else does that?"

"Uh, I do," Crystal puffed.

Spinach Alfredo pizza was a little slimy. It always got stuck in a person's teeth. The flavor of the sauce was rich, but it was bittered by the greens. Sylvia liked it. Crystal liked it, too.

"What went wrong?" Crystal asked.

She took deep breaths in and held them until the count of three before finally letting them go. Breathing so deeply made her belly puff out. It would have been unsightly if her shirt had been tighter.

"For one thing he opened doors for me," Sylvia began.

"Uh oh," Crystal shot back.

She was dead serious. Sylvia couldn't stand guys who held doors open. She didn't buy into that antiquated notion of a man being responsible for all the pleasantries in a relationship. She wanted equal footing. Sylvia might have let it slide once or twice because the gesture was polite, in and of itself, as long as he didn't get miffed if she returned the favor. If it became a habitual problem or if he huffed about a woman's obligation to subservient propriety, then her anger built up until it exploded.

"I know, right? Like I'm one of those wilting flower women. And he always had a story to tell and it was like I had to just sit and listen. And, on top of it, I had to think they were so interesting," Sylvia rambled on. Her face reddened around the edges. She swung her dangling feet violently against the edge of the table.

"*Were* they interesting?" Crystal questioned. She hugged herself. Her body slid lower on the counter, and she let the ledge bear her weight. The position made her legs looked stubby.

"That's not the point. I couldn't get a word in," Sylvia snapped.

"I can't see you putting up with something like that," Crystal agreed. She pulled her arms tighter against her body. The pressure was soothing. Her socking feet had trouble gaining traction on the freshly cleaned linoleum.

"It wasn't just little things. Let me try to wrap my head around it," Sylvia explained. She closed her eyes…

Chapter 2

TRUTH

The memories projected themselves on the back of Sylvia's eyelids like a movie theater. She and Jason were in his bedroom. His hair was unnaturally blonde, almost iced. He wore it short and spiked. If she touched the spikes with her hands they would sag and fall flat. He hated it when she did that, which made it all the more amusing.

When they first started going out, he straightened up before she came over. The whole house perpetually smelled like knockoff Fabreze. Fabreze was a lazy-man's air freshener to start with. It was designed to hide the fact that a person rarely kept up with housework. The telltale aroma told her to watch out. He was a closet-case pig.

Too much time had passed in their relationship. Miscellaneous, unidentifiable junk overflowed from under his bed. It spilled off of countertops like parachuting army men. He had settled into being a comfortable slob. It made her hate his face a little.

"I guess I felt like he was too…what's a good word for it? Squirrely? Yes, he was squirrely," Sylvia said, trying to explain the situation. She didn't really understand it herself.

She liked to go out. She didn't mind being seen with squirrelly Jason in tow if it meant she got to go out. The nights were more free and fun when she wasn't weighed down by the chains of looking after her purse. Sylvia was charismatic, but forgettable. Squirrelly Jason stuck out in a crowd, and not in a good way.

He seemed nice enough at first. Then he stopped trying. From there, it was a downward spiral of complacency.

"So he didn't know what he wanted?" Crystal asked.

Her voice was soft. From her position on the counter, some of her weight rested against the corner of the sink. A few stray drips of water soaked into her shirt and drew a small dark line in the center of her back.

"That wasn't the trouble. Actually, the opposite was true. Squirrelly Jason was too attached to me," Sylvia confessed. "His kisses were full of tongue—way too much tongue. They were the kind of kiss that makes a person want to throw up afterward. His hands would wander over my body when we were alone, no matter how many times I shot him down. I had grown to hate being alone with him. More and more, he wanted to stay in. He didn't feel like doing anything. I hate excuses. I hate lies. Jason was parrying for another chance to jab the back of my throat with his tongue. Maybe, he was finished doing the leg work with me, finished trying to impress me. Last night, I scoffed at the way we mysteriously ended up in a reclining position whenever we were together.

"'Let's lay on the couch.' 'It's more comfortable in my room.' 'I need to stretch out,'" she said, mimicking Jason. "He said a lot of stupid things in the guise of being smooth. His tactics were obvious. I'm not stupid. Apparently, Jason thought I was. When his moves failed to produce the results he wanted, he pulled me into his arms like a disobedient child. I hate his coaxing grin.

"I know I'm not easy to handle. I'm selfish, quick tempered. Hell, Crys, you know how I am. You're the only one who can stand me for extended periods of time. But this guy. At first, he seemed okay. Then it was always the Jason show. He was 'the man.' Right?" Sylvia flashed a glance at Crystal, who was watching her intently. When Sylvia looked at Jason, she got the impression he was drifting. He listened enough to track when to respond. But there was no genuine interest in his eyes. Crystal always put Sylvia first.

Sylvia tiptoed back into the memory. "We were in his bedroom. He pressed his body against me. I allowed it, but I didn't enjoy it. His sheets were thin and rigid. I wondered if he had stolen them from a hotel, or if he just had no money, coupled with bad taste."

Jason was supposed to meet Crystal in less than twenty-four hours. Crystal had asked to meet him. That was a big step for Sylvia. She couldn't say no. She could never say no to Crystal.

"I tried to enjoy Jason's company. He unbuttoned the first few notches on my blouse. For the first time in our relationship, I didn't stop him. Blood rushed from his brain to his face, among other places. I was bored, but he didn't seem to notice. That, more than anything, disgusted me."

"Put up or shut up. Isn't that what you say?" Crystal's said.

Her socks slipped on the floor. She scooted lower on the counter. If Sylvia had been watching, it would have looked like she was shrinking. Crystal wondered if she could shift positions without breaking Sylvia's concentration.

"I try to be compatible. Sooner or later my skeletons pop out of the closet and these guys aren't resilient enough to handle it," Sylvia guessed.

Crystal smiled at the imagery.

"It was his own fault," Sylvia continued. "Jason hasn't earned the right to touch me like that. In that moment, he was so unbearably pathetic. Heat spread over my body. Anger numbed the feeling in my hands. He didn't really listen to me. He didn't care about me."

Sylvia remembered that her hands had felt weak. She'd clenched both fists, but no matter how she squeezed them, they couldn't grip enough to satisfy her. Every nerve in her body had tingled. It felt like an electrical current. She squeezed Squirrelly Jason's arm tightly and flipped him over. His breath was shallow and labored.

She hated him. She hated the way he wanted her. Her hatred seethed until she'd hit him. Not just hit him. She'd punch him with all of her strength. The first blow landed square on his nose. Both of his eyes watered. She followed up with a few quick jabs. One connected with his throat. It was a solid hit, but his body had tensed so there wasn't much damage. He gasped. His mouth opened and closed. It had made him resemble a fish. Sylvia remembered giggling.

The passion of her anger filled her body. Vulnerability in his eyes made him appear more attractive than he had been a moment before. Jason knew how to push her buttons. He'd said he wanted it rough. The idea was exciting, so he grated on her nerves. His story was just like Sylvia's other boyfriends. It was fine in theory. He'd get bored with her weird fetish, or someone he knew would ask too many questions about the scrapes and bruises. Then embarrassment would lead to shame. Shame would turn into whispers behind her back until he decided he was better off without her. Sylvia had searched his eyes for signs of resentment after she punched him. There was something there, but she couldn't quite place it. She wondered if he was planning to ghost her without even the decency to break up properly. *Fine*, she thought. If that's what he wanted, then she'd give him something to remember.

"Well, you can always show your crazy face to me. After all, what is a best friend for?" Crystal asked.

She inch-wormed back up to a standing position, calculating the motion to be as subtle as possible. Sylvia's face was her spotting point.

"You don't have to worry about that," Sylvia responded. "That's the thing about skeletons. Everyone says they are no big deal, until they see one up close."

The popcorn was done. They let it sit in the microwave. Sylvia abandoned the memory and leaned on her elbows. The can of soda bubbled beside her. She rubbed her temples. The position covered her eyes with her hand.

Crystal let her gaze trace the curve of Sylvia's body. She was thin, but muscular, and tall for a woman. When she leaned back like that, her perfect breasts rose and fell with her breath.

Crystal stared silently. She wished she carried herself like that. She wondered why Jason would be stupid enough to break up with Sylvia.

Sylvia lowered her hand. Crystal shifted her gaze to

the tiles on the floor. Sylvia's shadow covered them in mystery.

"Headache?" Crystal said to the floor.

Sylvia craned her neck to one side. The bones popped. "Tension headache, my muscles are stiff and sore today." She smiled a crooked smile. There was something about her smile that made Crystal smile, too.

"Jason was dumb. I mean, you have everything going for you," Crystal assured her. She fought the urge to rub Sylvia's shoulders. If their roles had been reversed, Sylvia wouldn't have asked for permission.

Sylvia shifted her focus to the can of soda sitting beside her. She felt uncomfortable when Crystal praised her. She didn't deserve it. She wondered what Crystal would say if she told her the truth.

Crystal already knew that Sylvia had trouble controlling her temper. It should have been an obvious jump. Crystal wasn't like that. She was the type of person who only saw the good in others, whether it was really there or not. The problem was, it was easy to love someone at their best. Crystal was fragile. Sylvia had decided a long time ago that not telling her everything was the best way to protect her feelings.

Crystal counted Sylvia's positive attributes on her fingers. As she counted, she bent each finger farther back than was comfortable. The knuckles on her hand stung. Her voice was unsteady. "You're nice, hilarious, and drop dead gorgeous," she said.

"It's not me, it's you, right?" Sylvia's words were surrounded by laughter.

Even so, she looked a little depressed. *Maybe it is me,* she thought. It wasn't normal to beat on someone during sex, was it? No, she bet it wasn't normal. The look in Jason's eyes assured her of that. She pulled her chin down and slumped into herself, squishing her cheek against her shoulder.

The pose was uncharacteristically childish. It was adorable. Crystal tried to burn the memory into her consciousness. "Oh, come on. You just need to find someone who appreciates what a wonderful person you are. Someone you can spend time with, you know—like you can just hang out. Someone who knows you and won't judge you. Someone you can be on the same page with. Best friends," she suggested. She curled and uncurled her toes while she was speaking.

"You're my best friend, I don't need another one. Besides, where am I going to find a guy like that?" Sylvia asked. Crystal shifted her weight from foot to foot. She didn't have a good retort. Sylvia rolled her eyes. "Exactly. You go to a bar, you only meet guys who pick up chicks in bars. You get a job, you only meet guys who think they are better than you. You go to…God, I don't even know…a dating site, and you end up with some fifty-year-old nightmare, still squatting in his ancient gramgram's attic."

"You really need someone who doesn't get squeamish when things start to get serious. I'm sure the perfect person is out there. Any day can be the start of something special." Crystal stumbled over the words. They rolled around in her mouth before she could spit them out. Her tongue felt thick.

"Well, if you see the illusive perfect guy, then point him out to me, huh, Crys?" Sylvia raised one arm and made a gun with her fingers. She shifted it around the room and narrowed her eyes. Her sights landed on Crystal. "I don't want to waste my whole life hunting for a relationship that may or may not even exist." She pulled the imaginary trigger and let her hand kick back.

"There are nice folks out there. Look at you," Crystal said.

"More like, look at you. I'm not exactly easy to get along with," Sylvia answered.

She wasn't fishing for a compliment. She knew herself. She understood how people perceived her, and she accepted it. Her confidence was the best and worst thing about her. There was an arrogance to her strength that some people found abrasive.

Crystal opened her mouth to protest, but nothing came out.

"I'm lucky to have you. Maybe we'll end up like two old maids with all of these cats," Sylvia continued. Crystal frowned. "Like, so many cats that when we die, they eat our bodies for a few days before someone notices the smell," Sylvia continued. "No, wait! Let's get a monkey.

No one is going to screw with two old bats with a monkey."

"Speaking of eating people, I got some movies. Do you want to watch them, anyway?" Crystal pinched her lips closed and rested her tongue on the back of her teeth. It was a sudden topic shift. She didn't like it when Sylvia imagined her as an old maid.

"Hmm. What did you get?" Sylvia asked, her voice perking up.

They loved watching movies. Horror movies were a socially acceptable way for Crystal to be anxious. They were also a social accceptable way to appreciate violence.

"Well, I didn't know what Jas—everyone—would like so I got an action piece. It's very run-around-and-explode-a-bunch-of-junk. Hero stuff," Crystal said.

She crossed over and grabbed the bag from behind Sylvia. For a moment, their bodies pressed together. Crystal blushed. She forgot how to move. Seconds passed. She wondered how many was too many. She moved back quickly and fumbled with the bag. Sylvia's demeanor was unchanged. Crystal stared into the bag. She wouldn't have minded if it swallowed her head. Then she wouldn't have to make eye contact.

"Then—I—" Crystal stammered. "I got a horror flick about a killer on some kind of when-a-guy-falls-for-a-hooker-who-looks-suspiciously-like-his-sister rampage."

"Romantic comedy, huh?" Sylvia quipped. She let out a long, boisterous laugh.

Crystal's chuckle was more forced. It started out too loud, and then too soft. When Sylvia stopped, she took the cue to stop, too.

"You always know just how to cheer me up."

"I just love to see your smile," Crystal responded.

Sylvia hopped off the table and wrapped an arm around Crystal's shoulders. "Well, this one is just for you, Crys."

Sylvia used her arm to guide Crystal forward, controlling their speed and directionality. Crystal's arms were down at her sides. She was very aware of the space between them. The skin where they touched was warm. It tingled, even after Sylvia released her.

Chapter 3

CONFESSIONS

Movie credits scrolled across the television screen. Crystal and Sylvia sat on opposite ends of the couch. The popcorn bag rested between them. Sylvia shoved a handful of fluffy kernels into her mouth. They turned to face each other.

"Totally fake, right?" A few crumbs jumped out of Sylvia's mouth when she spoke. They bounced off of the couch and fell to the floor. Crystal pretended not to notice. Sylvia rolled her eyes. "I mean, did you see all that blood squirting everywhere? Totally unrealistic. If you got stabbed in the chest—" She pretended to stab Crystal in the chest with a closed fist. She was careful to stop short of Crystal's body. "—it would pierce your heart. Unless blood can magically pump itself without a heart."

Crystal gripped Sylvia's hand with her own. She squeezed. The back of Sylvia's hand brushed against her shirt. "Like you could even crack my sternum," Crystal shot back. The words were overtly gregarious. "Besides, I know when I get stabbed, I like to monologue for a bit before I start flopping around like a fish."

Sylvia pulled the popcorn from the couch and tossed it on the box table. Crystal scooted back and brought her knees up to her chest. She interlaced her arms around them. Sylvia spread her legs out to fill the gap Crystal left. She threw one arm over the back of the couch. The other draped over her knee.

"I'd just like to take this moment to ponder the cause of my imminent demise. Like—uh, no. I'd like to just take a minute to fight back. That's the trouble with people today. They have no fight in them," Sylvia complained.

Crystal leaned forward and put her hand over Sylvia's lips. Wisps of breath slipped through her fingers.

"Chloroform," Crystal whispered. Sylvia's lips were silky.

Sylvia crossed her legs Indian style. She thrust her arms into the air. "And another thing! Where does everyone get all this chloroform?"

"Uh, that's a good question," Crystal said. She stroked the bottom of her chin with her fingertips.

"Hello, I'd like to buy some chloroform please. Oh and maybe this duct tape, or some large plastic sheeting. 'Cause none of that screams psycho. I mean, what the hell else is a civilian going to use chloroform for?" Sylvia ranted. She was getting worked up. *Who sold that sort of chemical anyway, and how much is it?* She could think of about a hundred reasons she should own chloroform.

"Nothing. It's really toxic," Crystal answered.

Bantering back and forth like this made her feel in tune with Sylvia. When they were alone, they could meld on to the same page. Crystal lifted her arms into the air to stretch. The fabric of her shirt was pinned underneath her hips. Lifting her arms caused the shirt to flatten against her breasts. If the shirt was oversized, then her breasts were overstuffed. Crystal crossed her wrists above her head as she stretched to minimize the effect.

"It is?" Sylvia wondered aloud.

She tilted her head sideways. She had never heard anything like that. Of course, she was too afraid to have a search like that flagged on her Google history. She cracked the knuckles on her right hand. Crystal winced.

Cracking knuckles wasn't harmful. It sounded like it hurt. Really there was no underlying medical proof that it damaged the joints. She considered mentioning it to Sylvia. It wouldn't do any good. Sylvia cracked them as a side effect of her thought process. Most of the time, she didn't even realize she was doing it. Crystal shifted her focus back to the conversation at hand.

"Yes, ma'am. Chloroform can cause fatal cardiac arrhythmia. It can also cause depressed respiratory function or sudden cardiac arrest," she instructed.

She straightened up and shoved her hands into her lap. Her extremities were often cold. Heat from her lap soaked into her hands.

"Where did you hear that?" Sylvia asked.

It didn't seem comfortably within the realm of common knowledge. She rubbed the top of her knee with her hand. There was a small rip in her pants. The nub felt strange when she crossed her fingers over it.

"Internet," Crystal responded. "I did a paper on old-fashioned medicinal techniques and their updated versions in History 245."

She was pleased with herself. She liked being useful to Sylvia. She liked it even more that Sylvia trusted her word without questioning her sources. Sylvia would believe anything she said.

"I'll be damned," Sylvia said with a snort.

Crystal wasn't a bookworm, per se, but she was clever. She knew a little about everything. In school, Crystal hopped from subject to subject, never settling on any one area. Sylvia had always figured it was more practical to be an expert on one area, than to dabble. When a moment like this came around, it changed her mind.

"Well, it is still good if you don't care what happens to the person you use it on. Like Jason," Crystal commented.

She tried to be nonchalant. Talking about beating the tar out of her exes usually perked Sylvia up.

Sylvia hated hearing his name. Her hand curled into a fist. She smashed that fist into her cheek. Resting on it distorted the curve of her lips. Jason was a waste of time. He was a failure. In the back of her mind, she felt like a failure too because her love was so aggressive. *You can't just take a pound of flesh,* she mused.

Crystal started to speak, but fumbled over the words. "Yo—you.Y—you've got to fight for what you want. If you want to live—fight. If you want a woman—fight. If that were us, I would totally sweep you off your feet," Crystal avowed.

Sylvia smiled. She placed her foot over the top of Crystal's. Crystal's toes were frigid. It took conscious effort for Sylvia not to jump.

"In the movie," Crystal added quickly. "If we were in that movie, not like—I didn't mean if we were—you know—us. We are us. But if we were, you know. I don't know. Yah know?" Crystal turned toward the back of the couch and picked imaginary fuzz off of the upholstery.

"Crys?" Sylvia said.

The word was drawn out. It was slow. Her pitch dropped. She might have been talking to a spirited horse.

"No. Well, yes. I mean—that is what I said, but it isn't what I meant," Crystal said. She paused briefly. "If I was Jason, I never would have broken up with you. He was stupid."

"Calm down," Sylvia ordered.

She touched Crystal's hand so she would stop picking at the couch. It was sweet. Crystal was empathetic. She could see right through Sylvia's smoke screens. Sylvia's anger made her angry. Her sorrow darkened Crystal's mood.

Sylvia winked at Crystal. "I know exactly what you mean. You're my best friend. I can read your thoughts. You *have* to say what a fabulous catch I am."

Sylvia rubbed the back of Crystal's hand. Crystal had always been a picker. When she got nervous she picked at her clothes, her hair, whatever was close. She picked at the skin on her fingers. She didn't even know she was doing it. It was compulsive. Even with Sylvia's hand holding her steady, Crystal rubbed the fingernail of her index finger against the side of her thumb. A thin sliver of skin peeled up. Normal people would mistake it for a hangnail. Sylvia knew better. She gripped Crystal tighter. "It's really okay. I know you aren't exactly comfortable with all the dating talk, anyway."

Crystal's body sank into the couch. "I just don't like it when you're sad, Sylvia. I want you to be happy and find someone who makes you happy."

"Well you're the only person I haven't run off so far, Crys. So what does that say?" Sylvia joked.

"We are soul mates?" The words took Crystal's breath away. She had thought about saying it. They were the prefect words. Their friendship was the perfect ideal of opposites, yet they had similar interests and opinions. Crystal sat perfectly still. She was a deer perched on the edge of a meadow, peeking out to see if it was safe to move forward.

"You and me?" Sylvia didn't hesitate at all in her response. "Hell yea, we are. I wouldn't change it for anything. The guys out there are lucky you never date. I'd kill anyone who messed with you. It's flawless. I wouldn't hurt you. Not ever."

"I trust you completely, skeletons and all," Crystal murmured.

"That's because you know I mean it. If anyone mistreated you, I'd straight kill them," Sylvia confirmed. She released Crystal's hand in order to smack her fist into her palm to enunciate the words.

"When you talk like that, it sounds like you think we should run off together," Crystal mused.

She freely picked at the hangnail on the side of her thumb. It had always been this way, as long as she could remember. The jagged hangnail was ripping too deeply. It would bleed, but she couldn't stop poking at it.

"There's a thought," Sylvia said.

She returned her hand to its position on top Crystal's. Crystal seemed spooked all of a sudden. Sylvia wasn't good at reading emotions. She was even more inept at saying the right thing in tense moments. She smiled a wide, awkward smile. It wasn't an appropriate time to smile like that. Crystal scooted closer to Sylvia.

"I'm nothing like the guys you've dated," Crystal stated.

"You aren't a guy at all," Sylvia answered nonchalantly.

She glanced around the room. It was surprisingly bare. Crystal never accepted her offer to help out with the bills, or buy some more furniture. The room provided little insight to Crystal's shifting mood. It always looked the same. Sylvia wished they had more light than just the television glow to talk by. If she could see Crystal's eyes, then she might be able to tell what was bothering her.

"I know everything about you," Crystal commented.

From this distance, Crystal could smell Sylvia's shampoo. It was a lavender blend, sweet and subtle. It didn't suit her personality at all. Maybe, that's why Crystal thought it complimented her so well.

Sylvia paled. Crystal's words were almost true. Sylvia wished they were true. She wanted to tell Crystal the whole truth about Jason. A weak voice in the back of her head was screaming at her for lying. Lying to Crystal was unforgivable, even if she meant it as a kindness. Sylvia stared into Crystal's eyes—eyes flecked with evergreen. There was something behind Crystal's glance that Sylvia couldn't quite place.

She noticed that the space between them had shrunk considerably. She had been so lost in thought, she wasn't sure who had moved. Was Crystal closing the gap between them, or had she leaned in? Not knowing was uncomfortable somehow. The air was charged. Something was off. She felt inexplicably uneasy.

"Wait. Hold on. You almost sounded serious just then," Sylvia said.

Realization washed over her. Crystal withdrew. She scooted back as far as she could without physically getting off the couch. She grabbed the bag of popcorn and hugged it to her chest. An oily, stale scent filled her nostrils. It replaced the scent of Sylvia's shampoo.

"Hey, I'm just kidding. I mean you'd never be interested in that sort of thing for real. Right?"

Crystal kept her tone noncommittal. It could have gone either way. Sylvia widened her eyes. The question was a cross between a statement and a question. It gave Crystal room to backpedal.

"Are we having this conversation? Like you and me?" Sylvia asked. Crystal opened her mouth to respond. She hesitated. Sylvia jumped in to fill the silence. "You know, if I fell in love with you, it would end in disaster; like all my other relationship apocalypses. One day, I'd wake up and you'd be gone. I couldn't handle that."

Crystal sat up straighter. She stretched her arms so that her hands popped out of her shirt. "Hey now, give me more credit than that. I've been here this whole time, haven't I? I've been here watching you try to make it work with these guys. I'm the one who is here to pick up the pieces. I'm not saying we should go out," Crystal argued.

"You have always been on my side. I need you on my side," Sylvia said.

"Have you ever thought about it?" Crystal questioned.

Sylvia covered her mouth and shook her head back and forth. The truth was she had considered the notion—in passing. They spent so much time together. They got along. It only made sense that she should have considered it once or twice. Even so, she wasn't prepared for where this conversation was heading.

"No. Maybe. No," Sylvia faltered between honestly and safety.

A glimmer of hope shimmered in Crystal's eyes. In her experience, friendship was a fragile thing. Crystal liked the way things were. This was an all or nothing gamble. She didn't take chances very often. She didn't want Sylvia to look at her differently. She didn't want her feelings to ruin everything between them. Was the seed of doubt cast in Sylvia's mind? Could Crystal deny that she was in love with her? Her voice was barely audible when she responded. "That wasn't fair, it was..." She searched for the right words.

"Harsh?" Sylvia interrupted.

Her mind was racing. She expected to wake up. This was the part of the dream where they fell passionately into each other's arms, and then she woke up and laughed it off. She looked at Crystal. Quiet desperation replaced the normal serenity of her gaze. The way her eyebrows lurched together made lines across her face. The lines were full of fear and pain. Sylvia shifted her attention to the rip in her pants at the knee. Her own creamy skin was framed by the fabric.

"I was going to say selfish," Crystal admitted.

Her words triggered something in Sylvia that made her eyebrows shoot up. Crystal was a lot of things. She was caring. She was sweet to a fault. It was too easy for people to push her around. However, Sylvia always felt free to act like herself around Crystal. Crystal was a part of her, in a way that nothing else was. It frightened her. The thought of losing Crystal filled her with a panic she had never experienced before. If she didn't have Crystal, then she would cease to be herself. Crystal was a part of her heart—a larger part than she liked to admit.

"You aren't selfish," Sylvia deflected, only because she wasn't sure how else to respond.

"You are a woman who always does what she wants, no matter what. So what do you want?" Crystal was shocked by her momentary boldness.

Once the words started spilling out, she couldn't shut the floodgates. There it was, spewing out of her mouth. Everything she had fantasized about saying. It felt good. Like being drunk—feverish, giddy, exciting, and emotions she wasn't sure she'd ever felt before. It was empowering. However, a moment after it was empowering, it was terrifying.

"What do I want? A guy—" Sylvia started.

Crystal took a sharp breath and held it.

"—like you," Sylvia finished. She tried to avoid looking at Crystal when she spoke.

Crystal blinked. Her eyes were filling with moisture. The muscles in her throat melted closed. She could hardly breathe. "But not me?" she squeaked.

Sylvia could hear the tears in her voice. Knowing this made it harder not to look at her.

"I have you already, don't I? To be clear, you are telling me that you want to date me," Sylvia recapped.

There was no coming back from this. Everything was different now. Crystal had confessed her most embarrassing secret. Sylvia wished she could ignore it. She wished time would turn back so she could see it coming sooner. It didn't make any sense for Crystal to be attracted to her.

Crystal cried. It hurt. It hurt Sylvia's chest. She wanted to cry, too. She felt the tears raging behind her eyes. They wouldn't come. They never came. It made her heartless.

"No. I'm saying if you asked me to, then I would. I would do anything for you," Crystal said. Her voice trailed off and she stared into her lap.

"I will," Sylvia promised. She was pinned down, cornered between impossible choices.

Crystal's crying halted abruptly. Her eyes were bloodshot and swollen. She was a pitiful sight.

"I absolutely will," Sylvia repeated. "Just tell me when and where?"

Chapter 4

PREPARATION

Sylvia fluttered around her bedroom. Every so often she took a moment to move something a few inches. The next time she circled, she'd move it back. Her room was chaotic. Clothes littered the floor in piles.

Originally, one pile had been clean and the other had been dirty. Looking for specific garments had caused them to merge in the middle until nothing was either clean or dirty. Four bras hung off of her closet door knob. Every picture was covered in a fine layer of dust. Her mother's picture looked out from behind that dust, scolding the child she'd raised for slothfulness.

Sylvia hadn't told her mother about the date. The woman loved Crystal, adored her even. Crystal didn't have any family to speak of. It didn't take long before her mother had claimed her as a second daughter. The notion made Crystal nervous at first. Sylvia wasn't sure how her mother would react to the news. It didn't really matter either way. They never spoke about her romantic life. In Sylvia's mind, the woman was in complete denial that Sylvia was a grown woman now.

A stuffed animal rabbit sat on her king sized bed. He had both eyes, but the right ear had been partially amputated. His fur was matted down around the middle. Underneath a layer of time, he was brown. Now, he looked puke gray.

Sylvia had been ready for hours. A simple black dress hugged her body. It was low cut at the chest, but long and modest near the legs. It took two days for her to settle on it. Ruffles at the bust made her look fuller in the chest than she naturally was. Her hair was too short for an up-do, but she tried to twist it back. Scattered strands fell into her face whenever she tilted her head at a forty-five degree angle. She had three bobby pins clipped on to the back of her shoe in case it got too unruly.

Sylvia belly flopped onto the bed. Fredrick the bunny clung to the underside of her body. "This is stupid. Why am I doing this? It's so unlike me."

She flipped onto her back and held Fredrick up. He wiggled his arms and legs when she jostled him. She positioned one of his hands to the side of his face so he looked pensive.

"She gets to you. Nothing else has worked out. Maybe it's time to try something different."

Sylvia spoke in her normal voice. She never had much imagination when it came to that sort of business. Fredrick slipped out of her hands and fell on her face. His plush body gagged a frustrated sigh. She grabbed him and threw him over her head. He landed with a gentle thud.

"This is a bad idea."

She tilted her head toward the clock. Any minute Crystal would show up for their date. No one had ever picked her up for a date. She always met them. Rendezvous seemed sexier somehow. She wondered if this was how guys felt when they were waiting for her. She perpetually ran late.

Sylvia gave her armpit a quick sniff. The night hadn't even started. She failed the whiff test. She hopped up and walked to a chest of drawers. At first, she peeked over the top of each drawer to see if there was any deodorant laying on top. After that failed to produce results, she started rummaging. Rummaging gave way to a violent discarding of anything that wasn't deodorant.

She cursed and wondered why there was so much junk in her drawers. There was a pen. *Who needs pens in their bedroom?* She threw it on the floor. She tossed a length of rope, a hair brush, a whip, perfume, and a pocket calendar to the floor. If it wasn't deodorant, then she hated it. Perfume masked other smells, but it wouldn't help her sweating.

"Ouch!"

While moving things around, she sliced her finger on a knife in the third drawer. She tossed the knife onto an adjacent desk. It clanged. She touched her chin to her chest and smelled herself again. No good. The exertion was making it worse. She had begun to stress sweat. *At least with a black dress you can't tell*, she thought. Just when she was about to give up, she spotted the deodorant poking out from beneath a pile of clothes.

The deodorant was cold. She shivered when she slid the stick up and down against her skin. Sylvia rested her arms at sides. Moments later, she realized she was wearing black. When fabric touched wet deodorant it created a white stain. Immediately, she stuck her arms out like a bird and fanned her underarms with her hands. She checked and rechecked for white residue.

"I don't have time to pick something else," she lamented.

She peered into the dresser mirror. She looked ridiculous fanning her underarms. She turned sideways and ran a hand over her belly. *Does this dress really work?* She wasn't sure. Both hands cupped around her butt and smoothed the dress down. Black was supposed to be a slimming color. Her hips were too wide. Her mother called them child-bearing hips. Sylvia sighed. Even with the ruffles, her body resembled a pear.

She spoke frankly to the mirror. "You are thinking about this way too much. She's great, right? Right. And you care about her more than anyone else you've been out with so it makes perfect logical sense—logical sense. It's not like this is even a real date. You just couldn't stand to see her cry. You would never lose your cool with her, right?"

Sylvia paused. It was a possibility. Her love was overtly aggressive. Her feelings for Crystal were intense, even if they weren't necessarily romantic. Someone as soft as Crystal couldn't handle it if Sylvia went too far. She wouldn't do that. It was all about control. "Right. So why do I feel like I am about to throw up?"

The mirror didn't have a good answer for that one. She spritzed one wrist with perfume and rubbed it against her other wrist. Then she rubbed both wrists on either side of her neck so the scent wouldn't pool too strongly in any one spot.

Her finger was bleeding. A small streak of blood marked her neck. It served her right for keeping weird sex toys in her drawers. She pinched the finger against her thumb to isolate any further drops. There was no water or sink in her bedroom, so she licked the index finger of her opposite hand and cleaned the blood from her neck. It reminded her of the way her mother used to clean jelly off of her face. The spot turned red from rubbing it. It was obvious and awkward. Some ice from the fridge would help lessen the irritation.

"Sylvia? I knocked a couple of times, but you didn't answer."

Crystal's voice was on the other side of the door. Sylvia started cleaning frantically. After getting together a small armload of clutter, she thought better of it and dropped everything in a wad on the floor.

"Be right out, don't come in," Sylvia instructed frantically.

Chapter 5

DATING

Sylvia and Crystal arrived at the restaurant just after eight. They were seated quickly. Crystal was wearing make-up—eyeliner and lipstick, anyway. Sylvia had never seen her wear makeup before. If someone had asked her before tonight, she would have said that Crystal didn't own any except maybe Halloween nail polish. There was a magnolia pinned in Crystal's hair. Crystal had brought the flower to give to Sylvia. Sylvia had avoided the awkwardness of the gift by telling Crystal that it would look better on her than sitting in the apartment.

Crystal's dress was gray with embroidery along the

hem. It was form fitting, but modest in a way that Sylvia lacked. Sylvia was struck by how curvy Crystal was. Her own arms and legs were petite, to the point of seeming skeletal at times.

Crystal's feet, hands, and face were always cold and pale from the chill. Her waist tucked into itself in the middle. The curve of her breasts and hips made an hourglass. It wasn't a perfect hourglass. Her hips were small for her breasts. Crystal was far from being a pear. Sylvia blushed.

The greeter led them to a table in the center of the restaurant. Crystal felt like a spectacle. She preferred to sit in a corner, where her back was to the crowd. She tried to be brave. This was what she wanted. She had longed to be seen with Sylvia like this. In the center of the room, they would be unavoidable.

Crystal's hand hovered at the small of Sylvia's back as they walked. She willed it to make contact, but her nervousness wouldn't allow it. The restaurant was a quiet place, with only a handful of customers. They danced around the table trying to decide who would sit where. They opted for across from each other rather than side by side.

"I don't know what to say. This is weird. Is it weird?" Sylvia asked.

Crystal straightened the fork in front of her. She touched the tips of her fingers to her thumb. The taps bent in a line—index finger to pinkie and then back.

"Let's just talk about the same kind of things we always talk about," Crystal suggested weakly.

Things weren't going well. They weren't going poorly either. Sylvia's face was flushed. Her eyes jittered around the room.

"What's the point of going on a date if we just act the same?" Sylvia asked.

Crystal continued to tap her fingers while Sylvia spoke. This time the order was random. Even so, each finger got the same number of taps. Pinkie-middle-index-ring-ring-pinkie-index-middle. "I don't expect everything to be different just because we are on a date. I like the relationship we have. I don't want it to change, I want to add to it," she said.

Sylvia smiled. "That's actually really sweet, Crys."

Dark shading from Crystal's makeup made the green in her eyes appear more feline. Sylvia rested her hand flat against the table. The edge of her finger brushed against the place where Crystal's hand was resting. Crystal took the opportunity to interlace their fingers. Sylvia squirmed away.

"I'm sorry," Crystal whispered.

She looked around to see if anyone else noticed. She had a sneaking suspicion someone was scoffing at her feeble attempt at romance. Her eyes drifted from table to table. Each person was absorbed in their own evening. More than a few were talking or texting on cell phones instead of engaging each other in conversation. Crystal tried to remember the last time she saw a nontraditional couple on a date. No precedence came to mind, but it was hard to tell the difference in strangers.

"It's not that. It's just I hate having my pinkie on the inside," Sylvia explained.

Crystal raised an eyebrow. "Huh?"

"When I hold hands, I hate having my pinkie squished." Sylvia moved her fingers so that her pinkie was tucked in and Crystal's thumb was on the outside of her hand. She wiggled the pinkie to show how confined it was. "It's better this way," she added. She re-laced their fingers so her pinkie was on the outside.

"And I thought I knew everything about you, Sylvia."

"There is no reason for you to know this kind of stuff. Sometimes you show different sides of yourself to different people in your life. Not on purpose or anything. It's just force of habit. That's why I am not sure about all this, Crys."

Crystal was silent while Sylvia spoke. She soaked up her words and rubbed the side of Sylvia's hand with her thumb.

"You are the only person who calls me Crys, did you know that?"

Crystal's lips were pursed. There was very little room for the words to slide out. Sylvia shook her head negatively.

It was an unimaginative nickname. Most nicknames

ended up being the first syllable of a longer name. There was no one else to nickname her.

Crystal wasn't close with any of her family. Making friends had also proven a challenge for her. She couldn't sustain a normal conversation for long without devolving into a puddle of shyness. She needed someone who could monopolize the conversation and fill in the gaps. Approaching someone confident and outspoken like that made her uncomfortable.

Sylvia was about to respond when a waiter entered to take their order. The conversation entered into suspended animation while they made small talk and decided on the fly what they wanted.

Crystal ordered spaghetti and soda to drink. She fumbled a bit for the right terms, since she was more interested in the date than the menu. She asked what brand of soft drinks they had, but before the waiter could answer she asked him for, just a regular soda. "Whatever you've got is fine."

Even if she knew what brand they had, she wasn't focused enough to remember what products were included in that line.

Sylvia ordered chicken penne with lemonade and some water. She liked to dilute her lemonade with water so the flavor wasn't so overpowering. The waiter informed them they'd be allowed a salad and bread sticks to share.

"She doesn't like dressing. Can you bring the dressing on the side for me instead of putting it right on the salad?" Sylvia asked.

The waiter was cheerful. He was too eager to please her. Sylvia hated his face a little. He started to walk away.

"Not Italian. They default Italian dressing here. You have to ask if you want something else," Crystal said.

Sylvia stuck her tongue out. "Yuck."

Crystal hated Italian the least, since it was a thin, sparse dressing. Sylvia couldn't stand it. She wanted something creamier. Plus, if the Italian was too heavy, then the smell and taste would linger on their breath. Crystal had mints and gum tucked in her purse, just in case. The waiter offered them ranch.

"That would be great, thanks," the two replied in unison.

Mr. Waiter walked away, satisfied his gratuity was increasing.

"Was he staring, or was it just me?" Crystal asked.

"I would hate to be a server. They literally get paid to be nice to you. So whatever is happening on the inside, it doesn't matter. The nicer they are, the bigger the pay off. Typical," Sylvia commented.

She seemed a little more like herself now. She was loosening up enough to joke. Crystal stared at her from across the table. Sylvia's hair usually hung just above her shoulders. She alternated between chopping it bob short and letting it grow until she couldn't stand it. Now, it was just long enough to get in her way. She blew a piece out of her face. Her cheeks were red with anger at Mr. Waiter.

Crystal thought she was beautiful even when she was flustered. "Okay, how about this? Let's play 'what if.'"

The "what if" game was a sleepover party game that children played. Players took turns asking each other outlandish questions to try to evoke the best responses. Anyone unwilling to answer lost. No one really won. It was just an exercise in getting to know one another. It was a way to peer into the limited experiences of the players and try to take away something of how their mind worked. It was Sylvia's favorite game.

Sylvia smiled and leaned toward Crystal. "We haven't played that game in forever!"

"What if your eccentric uncle, Thaddeus, died and left you a fortune under the stipulation that you had to work as a waitress?" Crystal twirled a pretend mustache as she was talking.

"Okay, first of all, Thaddeus?" Sylvia giggled. "Who the hell was ever named Thaddeus?"

"We can make it Bartholomew if you want. Then you can call him Uncle Mew," Crystal suggested. She mewed twice like a cat and mocked a paw swipe in the air.

"If Uncle *Thaddeus*—" Sylvia emphasized the word to drive home how silly it sounded. "—left me a ton of money under the stipulation I work as a server, then I would spend all my time making up wild stories to tell my customers."

"Ooo, good one!" Crystal answered.

She was amazed at how quickly Sylvia could think on her feet. Sylvia was never at a loss for words. She always said the perfect thing. Ruffles on her dress swayed when she breathed. It made her breasts look like they were covered in black butterfly wings.

"One day I'd be a single mom with eleven children," Sylvia said.

"Planning to live in a shoe, are you?" Crystal commented.

"The next day, I'd be a sadist with a body count under my belt."

Sylvia got very still. She stopped smiling. Crystal didn't notice. Sylvia's hand tightened on Crystal's. It wasn't true. Sylvia had spoken without thinking, but it wasn't true. She wasn't a sadist, or at least not what she understood a sadist to be.

"What? Like, wake up the next day in a tub of ice, looking for a kidney?"

Crystal was obviously joking. There were teeth in her smile. She only smiled that big when she was having fun.

Sylvia withdrew her hand from Crystal's and clenched her fist. There was a little smack as she sat back in her chair. "No. Nothing like that."

She narrowed her eyes. The words slithered out. It

hurt. Sylvia understood how irrational she was being, but she couldn't logic away bruised feelings.

Crystal straightened her shoulders. "I don't think you have anything to worry about. No one would believe that, even from a millionaire waitress. Although, that kind of money would make body disposal a lot easier. You could have a mansion with a huge furnace." Her smile faded. Sylvia was dejected. It confused Crystal. Sylvia ate, slept, and breathed dark humor. She devoured it like candy. *Why the sudden change?* Crystal wondered. She tried not to read into it. Her shoulder blades spread. She breathed into the pit forming in her stomach and slouched forward. "We can stop playing."

"No. I'm just out of my element, I guess. I don't feel exactly like myself tonight," Sylvia said.

She reminded herself that Crystal had no way to know that her joking was equal parts saddening and enraging. Sylvia took a deep breath in. She used the breath to push her anger down. This was Crystal. She hadn't meant anything by it.

"It's your turn to ask me one, if you want to. Or we can talk about something else. You decide," Crystal offered.

She rubbed her hands together. They were empty. One was cold from where Sylvia's hand had been pressed into it. She looked longingly at Sylvia's hand. It felt like a step backward.

"It doesn't always have to be my way. Not with you.

We can still play," Sylvia answered. She took a few deep breaths. "What if you found the perfect guy, like the *perfect* guy?"

Crystal coughed awkwardly.

"Sorry! The perfect person. Nice and gentle. He loves you—he or she loves you." Sylvia fumbled over the words. "Gah, why am I making such an ass out of myself?"

Sometimes Crystal found Sylvia intimidating. Her grace, beauty, and strength were overwhelming for someone so naturally meek. When she saw Sylvia nervous, it made her feel more in control of herself and gave her confidence. "You are trying too hard. I think it's cute," she confessed.

"So this imaginary person is everything you say you want in a…partner. The kicker is, you can never have sex," Sylvia concluded.

"Nope!" Crystal answered. She waved a finger in the air playfully.

"What, nope? You can't just say nope. It's not an answer. Like, nope, what's the point of being with someone you can't have sex with? Or what?" Sylvia asked. She was speaking quickly. Her diction suffered.

"Nope, because you've asked me this once before and doubles are against the rules," Crystal reminded her.

Sylvia was caught off guard by her answer. It took some of the steam out of her. Crystal wrapped her arms around her own waist.

Sylvia's mouth hung open. "Huh?"

"They are your rules," Crystal said.

She could just barely see the tip of Sylvia's tongue behind her open mouth. She tried to remain focused on the conversation. Her tongue looked soft. Warm and soft. Crystal leaned forward. The edge of the table pressed against her belly. It was hard not to wonder what Sylvia's lips might taste like.

"I don't remember ever talking about this with you. We never talk about sex. I would definitely remember if we did. There are some good reasons we never have," Sylvia commented.

Crystal squirmed in her seat. The comment broke her fantasy. "It's not like that," she insisted.

She suddenly felt like a pervert. The truth was that she had always been attracted to Sylvia. Not just physically, but mentally too, and emotionally. She loved Sylvia's strength, loved everything about her. That didn't change the fact that moments before Crystal had been fantasizing about kissing her. Even now, she wondered how the ruffles on the top of Sylvia's dress would feel against her fingertips.

"Oh, not you. I didn't mean we don't talk about sex because of you, Crys—Crystal. God, what is wrong with me tonight? My hands are sweating and I can't even talk," Sylvia thundered. Her voice was loud enough that those closest customers turned toward them. Sylvia wiped her hands on the tablecloth.

Crystal half smiled. She pulled her teeth over her bottom lip. "Just breathe a second. I'll remind you. It was back when we first were getting to know each other. You were with that tall meaty guy with red hair. What was his name?" She paused. Neither could remember. "Anyway, he left you high and dry—up and disappeared. I picked you up at that hotel downtown."

"I sort of remember that. I can't believe you remember that," Sylvia said.

She often disregarded inconsequential things. She pulled at a necklace that was tucked into her dress and slid the charm back and forth against the chain.

"I only remember because it was the first time you spent the night at my place. Your eyes were so big. You had stopped crying before I got there, but the light made them sparkle. Your lips were puffy and swollen. You were a mess, the most beautiful mess I had ever seen..." Crystal recounted. Her voice trailed off.

Sylvia wasn't sure if she realized she had said the words aloud. Sylvia repeated the words to herself under her breath. "The most beautiful mess."

"You know me. If I found the perfect person, guy or girl, then I wouldn't let something like sex get in the way," Crystal said. She leaned closer so she could whisper the confession. "If I am being honest, I have never gone that far with anyone."

"So what if you get there and have no idea what you're supposed to do?" Sylvia said to herself.

Crystal grinned. "Hey, it's my turn to ask now."

Sylvia was seriously considering their compatibility. That was a good sign, but Crystal knew that Sylvia was high-spirited. It was best to let her acclimate to the idea slowly. The waiter returned with drinks and halted their conversation.

Chapter 6

SEDUCTION

S ylvia and Crystal approached the door to Sylvia's apartment. The sun had set. Shadows jittered across their faces as they walked. Their date was over. It felt surreal. Today, and everything leading up to it, could have been a dream. Sylvia opened the door and stepped into her apartment. The door wasn't open widely enough for both of them to fit through it. She stood with one hand on the frame, so the door was a barrier between them. Crystal leaned into the empty space so that Sylvia couldn't close the door outright.

"Can I come in?" Crystal squeaked.

Sylvia tapped her fingers against the door "Like

56

come in and hang out? Or like what's-the-color-of-your-bedroom-ceiling come in?" she accused.

Crystal felt a wave of nausea wash over her. In the first place, Sylvia's bedroom ceiling was white. Probably most of the bedroom ceilings in the world were white. She had seen it a thousand times. They had slept in the same bed. It had never been unsavory. Their friendship always mattered the most to Crystal. She never thought she would be brave enough to cross the line. That comfort in their friendship might be over now. Their whole friendship might be over now. It was shocking. Crystal's stomach turned. It was soured by Sylvia's accusation.

"I had a really good time on our date," Crystal whispered.

"I did too," Sylvia answered. She rested her head against the door. It was a narrow space to begin with. "I—I just don't want to give you the wrong i—idea," she stammered.

She felt shyness for the first time in her life. Her personality was big. Sometimes, it just started spilling out everywhere. Sylvia was prone to being rambunctious. She knew it. She'd never tried to be soft before. She had never wanted to feel timid. Crystal found a way to touch the softest parts of her heart. *How long can that last?* It was against her nature.

"We've been friends a long time. You know I wouldn't pressure you like that. I'm not some horny teenager, and I'm not a guy. Just Crys." Crystal gestured to herself. "I just don't want to leave without knowing how you feel. We work emotionally. We have the same sense of humor. After this date, I think we are pretty compatible. So what do you think? Is there something more?"

She looked deeply into Sylvia's eyes. It took conscious effort not to cast the look away.

Sylvia sighed, but relaxed the door. "We are great together. As friends. Companions. It all looks perfect on paper," she reasoned.

"I sense a 'but' coming." Crystal stated.

She wasn't sure how to live her life without Sylvia's friendship. She had never felt such a strong and volatile attachment to someone before. It couldn't be just her imagination. She was sure it couldn't.

"When I think of the relationship aspect, I can't handle it. You're like a sister to me. I couldn't act like I would with someone who isn't you. I wouldn't even know where to start. And if I lost you, then that would literally be it for me," Sylvia said.

She had always been blunt. If she ever censored herself at all, it was because she didn't want to be an embarrassment to Crystal. This wasn't a time to hold back. This was an all or nothing moment. If they were in for a penny, then they were in for a pound.

"How do you know you couldn't handle it? I mean we've never been in a situation like this before. I'll never leave you," Crystal stated.

She was calm. Her voice was firm. Sylvia's eyes wavered. Crystal knew Sylvia's heart. She pressed forward and filled much of the gap between them.

"I think that's why I am so uneasy. I feel so out of control right now. With guys it's easy. They are simple—mostly stupid—ridiculous creatures. It's so easy. Tonight, you are the one holding all the cards and I'm just wondering around in your shadow. I hate it. I love it," Sylvia contradicted herself. She felt washed away on a roaring tide. "I want—" she began. She opened her mouth to say more, but Crystal interrupted.

"Let me say something while I have the chance to say it. I may not be even close to your level, but I love you Sylvia. You are precious to me."

"My level," Sylvia laughed. "If you aren't close to it, then it's because you are so high above it. You're the one person I respect the most."

She went limp. Did she really feel that way? The men in her life had always been an annoyance. She tolerated them. She even liked some of the better ones. They'd had never been equal. Sylvia couldn't help but wonder if there was something wrong with her. *That is a horrible way to think, isn't it?*

Crystal took advantage of her dreamy attitude. "I'm going to kiss you, Sylvia. If you don't want me to, then you'll have to stop me."

The words were brazen. Crystal was already closing the space between them. There wasn't much time to react.

"Everything was perfect between us. Hot and cool. Calm and crazy. We balance each other so well," Sylvia blurted out.

Crystal hesitated. If Sylvia asked her to stop, she would have to.

"I can't catch my breath," Sylvia continued. "It feels like I am running and running just to catch up. I'm not this person, Crys. I can't change. I'm mean, harsh, and cruel."

"Don't say that, Sylvia." Crystal reached out her hand and caressed the side of Sylvia's face. "You may be all those things to other people, but not to me. Never to me. I trust you completely with my heart, my body, my soul."

Sylvia pulled away from Crystal's hand. "You shouldn't trust me. I don't trust me. I'll ruin it. I'll hurt you." Sylvia's words were passionate, like everything she did.

For once, Crystal didn't withdraw. She stood and fought for what she wanted. "It's my choice to take that chance, and I'm going to kiss you," she repeated.

She used the words as a pep talk. Sylvia started to shake her head no. Crystal pressed forward to see if Sylvia would let her through the door.

Sylvia hesitated, but didn't stop her from coming in. They faced each other. The door slid shut behind them.

Crystal moved toward her. Sylvia stepped backward, but there was nowhere to go. Her eyes widened. Their bodies touched from knees to breast. "Close your eyes for me? Before I lose my nerve," Crystal ordered.

Sylvia obeyed. She closed her eyes so tightly that lines formed in their corners. Her breath was rapid and uneven. Crystal was so soft. Sylvia was afraid to touch her. She was so small. Sylvia pressed her hands firmly down at her sides. Crystal was fragile.

"Forget for a second how complicated this is," Crystal whispered.

She ran a hand through Sylvia's hair. Sylvia felt like they were melting together. With their bodies so close, she couldn't tell where her skin ended and Crystal's began. Crystal's hand moved behind Sylvia's ear. She touched edge of her jaw with the back of her fingers. Sylvia wanted to cover her mouth. She was afraid what sort of sound might come out. Crystal's touch was like electricity seeping into her skin. The current ran around her body from the point of impact and radiated out.

"Forget all the reasons you keep trying to convince yourself this can't work." Crystal spoke the words like a magic spell.

Sylvia felt hypnotized. Crystal was so close that Sylvia could feel her breath on her face. She locked her elbows at her sides. Internally, she panicked.

"I love you," Crystal whispered. "Whatever you think your flaws are, I love them, too."

Sylvia licked her lips. They remained open a slit, inviting Crystal's kiss. They both inhaled deeply in rhythm.

Crystal kissed her. It was sweet and soft. She clung to Sylvia. There was strength in her tiny hands that Sylvia had never appreciated. It made Sylvia want to embrace her. Their mouths moved together, dancing around one another in flawless time. It was too much. Sylvia struggled to control herself.

She heard her own voice. It was something like a hum—a low-pitched sound that tapered off quickly. It should have been embarrassing, but it wasn't. She felt the corners of Crystal's lips turn up in a smile. Sylvia raised her hands and gripped the back of Crystal's dress. When Crystal started to pull away, Sylvia didn't open her eyes. Her cheeks were hot. She braced herself against Crystal, as if the whole world might be falling out from underneath them. Her lips tingled.

"I—I—" Sylvia was out of breath. Her mind was blank.

"Again?" Crystal panted.

Sylvia had no words to respond. The two came together again. Sylvia tried to be held. It wasn't in her nature. Her fingernails scraped across Crystal's back. Her dress was thick. She felt it, but it didn't hurt. Sylvia let her guard down. She nibbled the bottom of Crystal's lip. Crystal's cheek slid across hers. Her mouth went to Sylvia's neck. Her kisses were so soft they almost tickled.

Sylvia wrapped a hand around the nape of Crystal's neck. She took a loose handful of hair and squeezed it in her hand. Crystal took the cue and pressed deeper into her neck. Sylvia let her lips hover close to Crystal's ear. One excited breath after another pulsed across her ear. Sylvia's arms felt strained. She had no sense of how firmly she was holding Crystal. She bit the side of Crystal's neck. Crystal jumped and yipped, but didn't pull away.

"I can't—I can't do this," Sylvia panted.

The words were full of air. They packed no punch. Crystal didn't stop. Sylvia tried to pull away but there was no place for her to go.

"I'm afraid," she said.

Crystal froze in place. They both gasped quietly.

"I don't want you to stop," Sylvia's admitted. Her body was shaking. "I'm afraid."

Crystal held her tighter. "You are safe," she reassured her. She rested her chin on Sylvia's shoulder. "You are in control. You know I always do what you say. I can't help myself. Whatever you want. I don't care. As long as we can stay together, I don't care about anything else. I'll do whatever you want." She meant every word. It was easy to love someone at their best. Crystal bought out the best in her.

"Everyone says that because it's what I want to hear. But not from you. It isn't what I want to hear from you, Crys." Sylvia lost control of the volume of her voice. She shouted without meaning to.

Crystal offered a simple defense. "I'm not everyone."

"I know," Sylvia affirmed.

"My heart is yours. Whether you accept it or not, it'll always be yours," Crystal promised.

"I don't know. You don't know. If you knew—I have to tell you something. Right now. I've made up my mind. I have to tell you before it's too late," Sylvia said.

She took Crystal's hand and led her toward the bedroom. They closed the door behind them. Silence drifted around the rest of her apartment.

Chapter 7

BREAKING POINT

They sat. Sylvia gathered bits and pieces of what could easily be mistaken for a murder kit and placed them on the bed between them. While she was explaining what had lead up to her fight with Jason, her words were detached from the situation. She switched to passive voice several times and skipped the sexier details. They were implied.

Crystal didn't really want to hear that part, anyway. She listened quietly. She noticed that the bed was made. Sparkling white sheets peeked out from Sylvia's designer comforter.

Sylvia never kept her bed so neat, which meant she

had either gotten bored while waiting for Crystal, or she was concerned they might end up on the bed and wanted it to be clean. Crystal hoped for the later.

Sylvia squeezed her hands together. She told the truth, the whole truth. Fredrick the bunny acted shocked by her confession. The look in his eyes shamed her even more. Sylvia's breaths were tight. Crystal was silent. Her eyes were wide. Otherwise, her expression was void of emotion. The animation drained out of her. She looked like a broken doll.

It terrified Sylvia. "Please, say something," she begged. Her hands clasped tightly on her knees. The backs of her knuckles were pale from the effort. Sylvia moved as little as possible. She was like a child staring out the window at a lovely bird. She knew if she moved too quickly, it would fly away. "Say anything."

Crystal stood, shifted her weight back and forth between her feet, and tore at the skin on her finger with her teeth.

"Should I not have told you?" Sylvia asked. She felt an overwhelming urge to cry. She dug her fingernails into her palms. It stung. The pain acted as a gate to hold back the tears.

"I'm trying to understand what you're saying." Crystal's words were monotone.

"You think I am awful, don't you?" Sylvia asked. She pressed deeper into her palms. Moisture gathered in the corners of her eyes. She bit the side of her tongue and fixed her eyes on the floor. "Stop looking at me like that."

Crystal stared at her. Her reactions were delayed. After a few seconds, she blinked and breathed deeply. "Should I leave?" she asked.

She had intended to think the words and not say them. She was drowning in shock.

"No, please," Sylvia said. She bolted upright, took Crystal's hand, and interlaced their fingers. "We were having fun, right?" She held up their hands so that Crystal was looking at them.

Crystal shifted her gaze stiffly. "You're crying," she commented.

The words were matter of fact. A few tears had toppled over Sylvia's eyelids. Her vision was blurred. The rhythm of Crystal's words was off. The emphasis was placed incorrectly.

"What are you thinking? Please tell me. Are you afraid now?" Sylvia asked.

She was verging on hysterical, but quietly so. It wasn't the big, raging fit that Crystal was accustomed to. Sylvia was intense. Her world was crumbling around her.

"I've never seen you cry," Crystal mused. She noticed Sylvia's pinkie was on the inside of her hand. She wondered if she should fix it.

"*Is that all you can say?*" Sylvia belted out.

Crystal jumped. Their hands came apart.

"I don't know what to say," Crystal admitted. She

tapped her fingers together. The sequence was off and erratic. There was no continuity.

"I know it's not normal to hurt someone, especially during intimate moments. I know I'm not, right. But you said—you said we were soul mates," Sylvia reminded her.

Her makeup was ruined. She had never needed waterproof mascara before. Her eyes oozed black tinted tears down her face. They were years' worth of tears that she'd never cried. Once she started, she couldn't stop.

"So this is what a relationship is for you?" Crystal asked. She tapped her fingers more quickly together. She had a low tolerance for pain.

"No. I mean, this is what sex has been for me, or has brought out in me. I don't know if I've ever even been in a real relationship. I've never been with someone who mattered. You matter," Sylvia said.

"Have you ever—" Crystal started. A long pause drifted between them. Crystal wasn't sure she could understand it. She had never experienced anything like that before. She had never wanted to hurt someone, or something. In truth, she always made Sylvia kill her spiders. She swallowed. "Have you ever seriously injured someone?"

Sylvia dropped to one knee. She wrapped her arms around Crystal's waist. Crystal stood over her. Her spine was locked and rigid. Sylvia could feel the tension in her muscles. She was going to run.

"Define seriously. A broken nose, cracked rib, fracture fingers," Sylvia admitted.

Crystal pulled away. Her brain overloaded. She had been a weepy, wistful girl from the time she was small. The thought that someone would let another person crack their ribs for foreplay was disturbing. She couldn't imagine people with that sort of threshold for pain, or someone who could actually enjoy having their nose broken. Something like this could stop them from being together. Something like this might shatter her hopes for their future. It felt as if there was an animal in her chest, trying to claw its way out.

Not now, Crystal ordered her body. She was no stranger to panic attacks, but that didn't make them more manageable. Her medication was in the car. She couldn't breathe. She needed air. The walls of her vision started to move inward. Crystal left the room on autopilot. First, she looked for a window.

こうこう

A few moments later, Sylvia heard the front door open and close. The sound of a car engine roared faintly in Sylvia's ears. Slumping over on the floor, she curled up into a tight ball and laced her fingers in her hair. She spasmed and beat her limbs against the floor. One incoherent, roaring scream escaped her lips. After that, she sobbed quietly. Her eyes stared, unfocused, into the distance. Moments passed. She stood. Her reflection in the mirror caught her attention.

"I'm horrible," Sylvia told herself. She tried to get her breathing under control. "I'm worthless." She perched on the edge of the bed. 'She just—left." Her voice broke around the words. "Worthless. Horrible." Sylvia picked up the knife from the pile of items on bed.

She left. Without me, Sylvia thought. Her eyes traced the edge of the knife. She squeezed the hilt tightly. Her mood shifted. Despair didn't become her. Sadness wasn't in her nature. She scowled and clenched her teeth together. The sound they made when they grated was deafening. By sheer power of will, she steadied each erratic breath, forcing it to slow and focus.

She pulled the blade over her wrist in rapid strokes. Each swing made a puddle of oozing blood on her arm. She focused on the blade. It was slick and shining. The lubrication of the blood made piercing the skin easier. It was as if the tracks were already carved into her flesh, and she was just uncovering them.

She sighed. The pain validated her emotions. This was a pain she could deal with. Unlike emotional trauma, this pain was something tangible that she could process. She was in control of her body. A shallow nick here, a deeper slice there. Another, just enough to part the skin, like lips waiting for a kiss.

Sylvia liked symmetry. When she tried to grip the blade with her opposite hand, she had trouble closing her fingers around it. The knife fell to the bed. She tried unsuccessfully to pick it up. She could not close her left hand into a fist. Her body began to shake. She felt queasy, sluggish. Her head was full of concrete. The floor was hard, though she didn't remember falling. Her arm was pinned underneath her. It hurt. The adrenaline was fading. A searing pain invaded her tranquility.

ↄ⃫ↄ⃫ↄ⃫

Crystal drove, her hands pressed at ten and two. A seatbelt hugged her body. The brakes screeched. She unbuckled her seat belt, opened the door, and vomited into the street. She slumped over the steering wheel. Her hair fell across her face. *Silence*. She rolled her head to the side and accidentally honked the horn. Her shoulders jumped skyward. Her foot pressed the gas petal, but she was still in park.

"Calm down," Crystal ordered herself. Her voice was firm. She wiped her eyes and face. *Breathe*. Sucking air in through her mouth, she let it cloud out of her nose and held her hands in front of her—palms out, fingers spread. "Calm down."

Her purse lay next to her on the seat. She rummaged in it until she found a tissue and wiped the corners her mouth. While feeling around, she bumped her cell phone. It lit up. She snatched it out of habit. Her screensaver was a picture of Sylvia.

"I am driving, where am I going? What the hell am I doing?" She started punching numbers on the phone then hit "End" instead of "Talk."

Sylvia's phone was sitting on the floor of the living room.

Crystal dialed again and let the call ring through. She tapped her fingers on the steering wheel in order. No answer. She hung up and called back. No answer. One more time, but this time she left a message.

"It's me. I—You—Just call me back." Crystal took the phone away from her ear to hang up, stopped to think, and put it back up to her cheek. "Are you angry? I needed some air. God, you're probably so pissed. Call me. I'm not sure where I am, or how to get back. Please let—" The time allotted for the message was up.

"If you are satisfied with your message," the voice-mail robot said.

"Shit!" Crystal tossed the phone on the dashboard. She leaned against the steering wheel. Sylvia and she had never had a fight before. Sylvia had never been angry at her before. Maybe, she wouldn't want her to come back. Crystal felt like a fool. It made sense. It fit. So why hadn't she ever noticed before? Sylvia had trusted her completely for the first time. Crystal smiled. Strands of stray hair fell across her face and shadowed the smile. It would work out. They were soul mates.

Chapter 8

TIME

Crystal remembered that night in vivid detail. She had wandered for twenty minutes before she found her way back to Sylvia's complex. She stood at the bottom of the steps leading to Sylvia's door. A sour taste pooled in the back of her mouth. The back of her throat still tasted like vomit. Burning soreness from stomach acid crept into her esophagus. She took a single step toward the door.

Crystal had rushed to get back. Her car drifted toward the curb as she sped around corners. The back right tire scraped against the concrete guidelines of the road. Her body had swayed with the sharpness of the angle.

The carelessness of her speed got her more lost. Sylvia's neighborhood was nicer than hers. The houses were bigger, though clustered farther apart. Condos and apartments were trimmed identically. From the street, it had all looked the same.

Now that the door was so close, Crystal hesitated. She was starting to wonder if coming back was the right thing to do. She thought about the moment when she told Sylvia about her attraction. Confessing something so monumental was like ripping the scab off of an old wound. It hurt. It burned inside like a slowly roaring fire. Yet, if the scab never came off, then the secret festered. It rotted all of the healthy skin around it until everything was consumed.

Crystal leaned against the bottom of the staircase. Sylvia would be angry. Crystal forced herself to lift her foot off of the ground. The bottom of her shoe scraped along the fluffy carpet in the hallway. She could feel the skin of her back pull tight. Her collar bone sank into her chest. It created a divot just the right size for her chin. She tucked her head sideways into the space.

Crystal knew what Sylvia's anger looked like. Sylvia had a short fuse. She was a force of nature when she lost her temper. Crystal was awestruck by the tenacity of her fury. However, because it burned so hot, it usually fizzled out after a short duration.

Up until that moment, Crystal had always been standing behind Sylvia while her anger was directed at someone or something else. She had never been in the line of fire.

Crystal took off her shoes and tiptoed to the door. Her fingers spread out in thin lines against the eggshell paint of the door. The door had been painted and repainted so many times that it felt unnaturally thick under her hand. She pulled her hair around her neck and pressed her ear against the door. The room inside was quiet.

Sylvia always called Crystal when she was upset. The silence behind the door was jarring. Sylvia didn't have anyone to call about this. Crystal was the person she confided in. There was too much to explain to anyone else. It was a long, awkward series of events. Sylvia's mother wouldn't understand. Her sister lived across an ocean and had no idea who she was anymore. Sylvia was fiercely competitive with her other friends. Showing them any sort of weakness was out of the question.

Crystal guessed Sylvia didn't put enough stock in their advice to explain it all in detail. At the end of the day, Sylvia wasn't attracted to women. Crystal couldn't pretend otherwise. Everything in their history suggested it. However, she wasn't really attracted to men either. Sylvia had practically told her that, barely an hour ago.

Crystal tapped gently on the door, fighting the urge to scurry away. Sylvia would yell at her.

Crystal should give her that chance. She deserved a sound scolding. It would loosen up the knot of guilt forming in her belly. Sylvia's wrath would ease the wave of self-hatred washing over her. Everyone would feel better after.

Crystal practiced her apology. She played out in her mind what Sylvia might say and what her answers might be. In reality, Crystal would probably just sit there and let Sylvia scream at her. It was foolish to presume she'd defend her actions. Sylvia hated excuses. Then again, she was well versed in Crystal's panic attacks.

It was possible she would be more annoyed than angry. If they let the sun go down on an argument, it might disenchant Sylvia with their date. It had to be now. Crystal couldn't take that chance.

The doorknob circled callously in her hand. It gave no notice of the horrible scene awaiting Crystal's arrival. She stepped into the apartment. It was dark. She expected it to be a mess. Sylvia threw things when she was upset. She knocked things over. Everything was as Crystal had left it. The apartment was wrapped in stillness.

She lost her voice. She didn't remember screaming, but her voice was hoarse for three days after.

☙☙☙

They wouldn't let her sleep with Sylvia at the hospital. They wouldn't let Sylvia have any visitors at all. The couches in the waiting room were too small to comfortably sleep on. The night it happened, Crystal dreamed about trying to hide suspicious objects before the ambulance arrived. In the dream, she pressed her knees onto Sylvia's arm. She wasn't strong enough to apply pressure with her hands alone. She was too weak.

Crystal wound a shirt around Sylvia's arm and shoved anything incriminating she could find in between the box spring and the pillow top. There was blood on her hands. There was blood on her lips. She'd kissed Sylvia frantically. But Crystal was calm in the moment and did what needed to be done.

⁀ɔc⁀ɔ

Now, weeks had passed. Sylvia was home. Her arm was bandaged during the day, open to breath at night. Crystal had creams and lotions to put on it. They littered the bathroom countertop. It was the only outward sign of what had happened. Sometimes, it did seem like just a bad dream.

Sylvia sat upright in bed with her laptop. The injured arm hung lifeless across her chest. She propped a pad of paper and a pen on a pile of pillows. The covers were a mess. They were bunched up and disheveled. Sylvia's feet stuck out of the bottom of the blankets. She typed on the computer one-handed. Her eyes tracked along the screen. Every so often, she grabbed the pen with her good hand and jotted something down. Her handwriting was sloppier than ever. The laptop teetered, unbalanced.

Crystal burrowed into the covers and cuddled up to

Sylvia's side. Crystal was wearing pajamas with black cats on them. Sylvia's—now their—apartment was drafty. Crystal had always had trouble staying warm. Sylvia liked air flow when she slept. She wilted like a flower in the heat. They bought Crystal a pair of pajamas for every night of the week to make up for the chill. Sylvia was sweating a little in only a bra and panties.

"You are still awake?" Crystal asked.

Sylvia dropped the pen and patted the top of Crystal's head with her uninjured hand. "Is the light bothering you?" she asked, but she didn't stop reading.

"No," Crystal lied. She yawned and wrapped an arm around Sylvia's belly.

"But, really, it is?" Sylvia guessed. She kissed Crystal's hair.

Crystal's eyes were closed. She smiled gently. "What are…" Her voice was low and sleepy. She trailed off.

"Just thinking," Sylvia stated.

Sylvia was an insomniac. Once she fell asleep, she could sleep all day. It wasn't uncommon for her to sleep ten or twelve hours at a time. The tricky part was falling asleep. Her mind was restless. She was too focused to relax. It took her a long time to wind down. She raised her injured hand. It took effort to straighten her fingers at all. She held the position for a moment before the hand returned to home position.

She sighed. "I have to figure out what to tell the shrink in our session tomorrow. I'm thinking about going for situational depression, but the symptoms I'm seeing are just too variable. I don't want to get something like bipolar or schizophrenia," she complained.

Crystal was trying to stay awake and listen, but she drifted in and out of the conversation. She gently rubbed the skin on Sylvia's belly with her thumb. She "Mm hummed" lightly in response.

"Really, anything without violent tendencies shouldn't follow me around. Maybe, I'd be better off taking a drug angle. I don't know. Those programs attract a lot of attention too," Sylvia said.

She tried to use her injured hand to pick up the notepad, but couldn't. Crystal breathed deeply.

"If I can trick him into a solid diagnosis, then I shouldn't have to keep going back," Sylvia huffed.

She stuffed her injured hand under the notepad. When she tried to lift it, her fingers gave out. Crystal opened her eyes when the notebook fell to the sheets.

"Voluntary, my ass. Sometimes, I just want to kill that guy." Sylvia followed the words with a deep, gruff exhale.

"What does he look like?" Crystal demanded. She frowned and sat up. Her attention was focused now. The blankets fell around her. A cold breeze washed over her and made her body shiver. She wiped her eyes.

"Huh?" Sylvia asked. She fumbled to try and move her research materials out of the way.

"This guy, your therapist, what is he like, anyway?

You've never talked that way about him before," Crystal said.

Sylvia closed the laptop. She guided it to the floor and turned to face Crystal. Crystal's eyes were narrow and sleepy. Her hair was flat from the blanket cocoon she hibernated in. Sylvia's eyes adjusted to the dimness of the room. "I didn't mean it that way, Crys."

"You may not have 'meant it,' but it *is* what you said," Crystal huffed.

She threw herself back into the covers. The motion put distance between her and Sylvia. Sylvia reached out and loosely gripped the shoulder of Crystal's pajamas. The angle sent little jabs of pain up her arm. She wanted to turn Crystal over, but didn't have the dexterity. She rested her chin on Crystal's shoulder.

Warmth radiated from her body. Crystal wished it didn't feel so good.

"I want to kill him—like I am frustrated, not like I actually *want to kill him*." Sylvia emphasized the second part of the phrase. She decorated Crystal's shoulder with a line of kisses.

"Have you thought about him that way?" Crystal asked.

Sylvia hesitated. The first rule of relationships was don't talk about your ex unless you want to fight. The second rule of relationships was don't talk about anyone who could be seen as a rival. Crystal was insecure. If she said no, then Crystal would assume she was lying. If she said yes, then it would crack her already fragile self-esteem.

Crystal exhaled out of her nose in a rough snort. "Well?"

"He is nobody. He is just some arrogant guy who thinks his opinion is important just because someone told him he could put the word doctor in front of his name," Sylvia said before resting her hand on the dip above Crystal's waist.

The intimacy of her touch made Crystal squirm. "Sounds like your type. You always like to put guys like that in their place," she said.

When Sylvia touched her, it was difficult to focus on anything else. Crystal's commentary was completely accurate. He was her type. He was handsome too, in his own way. None of that made any difference. Sylvia wasn't that person anymore. She could hardly move her hand. The prognosis wasn't great—pain, numbness, a difficult rehabilitation that might not help at all.

Sylvia nibbled lightly on Crystal's shoulder. "Don't be that way."

"Do you think that way about me?" Crystal asked.

She was serious now. A grave look glossed over her. It made lines in the corners of her mouth. Sylvia thought she was too fair and too lovely to look so serious.

"No," Sylvia responded.

There was no hesitation. She shook her head firmly enough that it shook Crystal's shoulder where they were touching. Sylvia brushed Crystal's hair with her fingers. "Not even a little bit."

Crystal sulked. "Do you think you'll *ever* want me?"

She tried not to let it bother her. It was going slowly. Most days they had fallen back into the pattern of best friends, sisters, or roommates. That sort of relationship was charming and wonderful in its own right. At the same time, they were all of those things and none of those things.

Crystal wanted to do more for Sylvia. She hated her stupid cartoony pajamas and the way they undermined her position as a woman.

"No. I'll never want you like that," Sylvia confessed.

Her voice was soft and gentle. She nuzzled into Crystal's hair and breathed her scent in.

Crystal pulled her legs up so she was scrunched in a ball. Sylvia spooned her body around Crystal and rubbed the outside of her leg. Crystal shivered a bit from being out of the blanket. "You barely know this guy, Sylvia."

"You're reading too much into it. You don't want me to feel that way about you. You don't want me to hurt you, do you?" Sylvia questioned.

There was silence. Crystal rubbed her feet against each other. Her ankles knocked together when they passed. She pulled the covers up to her nose. "I guess not. But I want you to want to," she said.

She hid her face while she was talking. It was embarrassing. It didn't make sense. She had a very low tolerance for pain. It was hard not to feel like something was missing between them.

"Well, I don't. I don't want to and I don't want to want to," Sylvia reiterated.

Crystal craned her head around to look at Sylvia. Her panties were black. There was a fringe of lace around her hip that trailed down into the depths of her thigh. All of her underwear was like that.

Crystal looked at her pajamas. "If you wanted to try—" she started, but Sylvia interrupted her.

Why did so many of their conversations end this way? Sylvia's voice shifted to a firmer, more aggressive tone. She was louder, her muscles tensed. "I said, no. That means, no, Crys."

Crystal pulled the blanket completely over her head.

Sylvia pulled down the blanket and kissed the tip of her nose. She softened her voice. "We will get there. I want *you*. I can't hurt you. Not ever. Not even once. We will—" There was an awkward pause. "—get there."

"Promise?"

Crystal felt herself yielding. She remembered how sleepy she was. Sylvia looked over her body. There was nothing condescending in her glances. She saw Crystal as a woman. The look in her eyes was a modification of a best friend. It was more intense than that. Crystal breathed deeply.

Everything was going well, just slowly. Crystal reminded herself that there was nothing wrong with easing into everything. Sylvia always went at her own pace.

Sylvia playfully smacked Crystal on the butt. "Of course! You are super-hot. All the guys are jealous of me."

"If you aren't ready, I don't want to pressure you. I know your arm—" Crystal swallowed her words.

Sylvia stiffened. They didn't talk about it. They never talked about it.

"That has nothing to do with it," Sylvia said.

Her words carried with them a sense of finality. It was not up for discussion. Crystal sank into the bed. She wriggled a bit, her eyes round.

"I love you," Sylvia said. "You know, you're cute when you're jealous."

Crystal pouted. "I'm not jealous."

Sylvia pressed her mouth against Crystal's. If there was more to say, Sylvia wasn't going to let her.

"Then you're cute when you're not jealous," she whispered.

Crystal couldn't help but smile. She cuddled back into Sylvia.

Chapter 9

THE HEART WANTS

Crystal woke up early in case Sylvia needed any help. Sylvia never asked for help. She probably didn't want it. Crystal was working out a system of secretly caring for her, without hurting her pride. The house was empty. She had missed her chance again.

Crystal spread herself out on the couch and read a book. Sylvia had a real coffee table, so when they merged their stuff together, the box table had been thrown out. At least, Sylvia tried to throw it out.

Crystal rescued it from the trash and was hiding it in the downstairs storage area with other items that wouldn't fit in the apartment. There were too many memories to let

it go so easily. Of the two of them, Crystal was senti-
mental.

She was wearing a blouse suitable for going out, but
she had the same adorable pajama bottoms from the previous night on. There was a general level of clutter
around that room that would normally have made Crystal
uneasy. It was Sylvia's clutter. That made it feel like
home. The "Crys's junk box" sat on the floor in one corner next to a "Sylvi's junk" box. The writing on the box
was small and cursive. Crystal sprinkled pictures of the
two of them on walls in between Sylvia's pictures of her
family. The pictures weren't all straight or logically ar-
ranged. Adding frames without reorganizing the whole
wall left some of them askew.

Crystal heard noise in the hallway. Sylvia struggled
to open the door. Crystal hated herself for forgetting to
unlock it before Sylvia got back home. She meant to, she
even thought about doing it, but the time slipped away
from her. If she did it now, then it would be too obvious.
Crystal swore mentally to make it up to her.

When Sylvia entered, Crystal jumped up and threw
her arms around her. "Welcome home," she exclaimed.

They kissed. Sylvia smiled and wrapped her arms
around Crystal. She picked her up off of the ground and
swung her back and forth. Her feet dangled. Crystal was
petite—light as a feather.

Even so, it hurt Sylvia's arm to bear her weight. She
turned her head sideways so that Crystal wouldn't notice

the pain on her face. Crystal glided back to a standing position.

Sylvia let her purse fall to the floor. "I wasn't gone long," she said.

"No, but I know you really didn't want to go," Crystal answered.

She picked up the purse and set it on a table by the door.

Sylvia noticed the book, walked over, and picked it up. "I hate that man," she muttered under her breath.

She flipped her tongue around the words. Crystal slid Sylvia's coat lower on her shoulders. It was too warm for a jacket, especially for Sylvia. She wore it because it was difficult for her, to prove to Lee that she could. Sylvia opened the book with one hand and looked at it.

"How long do you have to keep going? I mean no one ever said you had to go," Crystal commented.

She tugged on the sleeve of Sylvia's coat until her injured arm was free. Next, she took the book from Sylvia and held it so she could still read it while she pulled the other arm out of its sleeve. Sylvia was too preoccupied to object. Once her coat was off, Crystal put the book back in Sylvia's hand. She went and hung the coat on its hook.

"Not much longer," Sylvia said. She read a few passages quietly. "He wants to help people. He doesn't say it, but I see it there behind his stupid, brown eyes."

Crystal popped back into the room, sans coat. They

both sat on the couch. Crystal wiggled under Sylvia's injured arm and held the book while they both glanced over it.

Sylvia's blue eyes skimmed the pages twice as fast as Crystal's green ones. Sylvia nudged Crystal. Crystal narrowed her eyes at the page. She dragged her teeth across her lip. Sylvia nudged her again. She turned the page even though she wasn't finished reading. Her eyes followed the last few lines until they were no longer visible. She gazed at Sylvia instead of the pages.

"A real knight in shining armor, huh?" Crystal asked.

She wondered why Sylvia was more willing to talk about him in daylight. Just hours before the topic had been off limits.

"He is detached too, though. It's so infuriating. I can't decide if he has me totally figured out, or if he is clueless," Sylvia hissed.

She kicked off her shoes. One of her socks slipped down on her foot. She tried, unsuccessfully, to pull the saggy fabric up with her toes.

Crystal leaned down and pulled on the toe of her sock until it came off. She removed the other sock as well. Sylvia started to frown until Crystal placed the socks on her own feet. She wrapped her hands around her feet like she was making the socks hug her fingertips. She was smiling. Sylvia smiled too. The socks were too big for Crystal. It made her like a little girl playing dress-up in Mommy's shoes. Sylvia wondered in passing if her own feet were mannish, or if Crystal's were tiny.

"What did you two talk about?" Crystal asked.

"About how helpless I am now. I need someone to tell me I am strong so I feel better again," Sylvia said.

She took the book from Crystal and tossed it on the floor. It landed so that the pages were bent. Crystal stared at it. She worked at the library. They gave her an extension on it without making her come in because of everything that had happened. The book would never shut properly again. The two shifted positions so that Crystal was sitting and Sylvia was lying down, with her head in Crystal's lap.

"I'm surprised you could fake that," Crystal said.

She touched Sylvia's head. Sylvia's hair was full and fluffy. It must have rained during the night. Sylvia turned her head and snuggled underneath Crystal's breasts. She held her breath. Crystal blushed. There was silence. Moments passed.

"Come out of there," Crystal pleaded. Sylvia shook her head negatively. The force of her nod wiggled Crystal's breasts. Sylvia burrowed in farther. "Sylvia, can you breathe in there?"

Sylvia answered, but her words were muffled, inaudible speech. She relaxed and took a gasping breath. She inhaled and tried to sneak back into her, under her bust, but Crystal gently pushed her head back down into her lap.

"Oh come on," Sylvia begged.

Crystal responded by hugging her head tightly. "Was it that bad?" she asked.

She looked down at Sylvia. Her eyes were dark around the edges. They looked a little puffy: swollen from over wakefulness.

"Yes. His superiority complex makes me feel like crap sometimes. I'm a small, beautiful, doll to set on the top shelf where no one can reach it," Sylvia said. Her voice changed. She intended to mimic Dr. Lee. Of course, he had never said anything like that to her. What came out was a cross between her natural speaking voice and her "dumb guy" voice.

Crystal could see why Sylvia hated Lee. She hated him, too. He made Sylvia unhappy. For some reason, for the time being, Sylvia felt obligated to let him. Crystal wondered if they talked about her. She wondered what Dr. Lee said about their relationship. Pangs of jealously edged into Crystal's mind. She wished she could see them interact.

"Beautiful, yes. A doll, no. Although, that is wonderfully macabre. At least sound like yourself," Crystal said.

Sylvia stuck out her tongue. Crystal answered by sticking out her own tongue. They leaned forward and touched the tips of their tongues together and then relaxed. "Your check came."

"Stupid settlement," Sylvia snorted.

A rough breath floated out of her nose. Sylvia had accepted a settlement offer from her previous employer to make a problem situation go away. She had been the problem.

"I thought you'd say something like that, but I booked our cabin with the money!" Crystal squealed.

She pressed her hands together, palms in, like she could be praying. Then she turned her hands toward her body so that her fingers were pointing toward Sylvia. It looked uncomfortable. She rested her chin on the heel of her hands.

"You did?"

Sylvia was distracted. Her question betrayed how oblivious she was to Crystal's excitement. She looked at her hand. Her fingers were slightly curled in. They sat in home position. At times like this, Sylvia wondered if the hand was even a part of her body. She expected it to crawl away on its own. She was sure that one day it would pop off and Crystal would have to chase it with a broom as it scuttled around the apartment. Crystal picked up Sylvia's hand and laced their fingers together.

Crystal smiled. "It's just what you need, Sylvia. You love going to the lake. We'll watch a couple of movies. The woods are totally freaky. It's going to be awesome!"

"There is no AC. Last time we went, I was so hot I couldn't breathe," Sylvia complained.

She kissed the back of their joined hands. The position pulled Crystal's hand farther down than was comfortable. She had to strain the tendons in her wrist to accommodate it.

"I'll pack a fan, and we can run around in our underwear," she teased.

She raised an eyebrow in an attempt to look alluring.

Sylvia worked hard not to laugh.

"Maybe it will be fixed this time," Crystal said. "I got the bigger place way on the edge of the property."

"If the fan is on, we won't be able to hear all those axe murderers coming to get us," Sylvia stated.

She let out the laugh she was trying to pin down. Crystal didn't exactly scream confidence. Sylvia wondered if this was a sex trip. The thought didn't bother her as much as it should have.

"That's my girl, beautifully macabre," Crystal said.

"Are you nervous?" Sylvia asked.

She felt awkward bringing it up. They were making progress being a couple. The whole concept was so foreign to Sylvia. Not just because she was aggressive. She wasn't entirely sure how two girls had sex with each other. She nibbled on the side of Crystal's hand. Crystal smiled sweetly and missed the point entirely.

"Nope. I don't think there really are axe murders in the woods anymore. Probably bear attacks and stupid policemen," Crystal said.

Sylvia sat up. She put some distance between them. For a moment she was very quiet. She picked at the nails on her left hand. Her nails had fallen into ruin since the accident. She had two unsightly hangnails that she always forgot to clip. The hand was still fairly numb. She had picked them bloody on more than one occasion without realizing it.

Sylvia ran a hand through her hair—backward, starting from the nape of her neck and running up to the top of her head. A lock snagged on the jagged skin on the side of her thumb. She shifted her weight to one side. It was better if it was spontaneous. Talking about it wouldn't have done any good anyhow. It was supposed to be fun.

"Coyotes more likely," she commented.

Chapter 10

THE TRIP

The next few days were full of packing. Crystal did most of the work collecting things. It wasn't that Sylvia couldn't do it, it was more that Crystal had a head for where everything was in the apartment. She had unpacked most of it before Sylvia had recovered from that night. Sylvia had come straight from the hospital. Their Frankenstein apartment awaited her.

They crammed the car full of bags and suitcases. Most of the contents were neatly organized on the right hand side of the car. All of the suitcases were stacked by size. The other side of the car was full of bags. There were some grocery bags with snacks and dry goods, some larger bags full of clothes, and a small laundry basket full of miscellaneous toiletries. There was a brightly wrapped wine box nestled safely, but hidden, amongst the piles.

Crystal drove. She drove for so long that her legs were stiff. Her butt hurt when she moved and was tingly-numb when she didn't. She shifted her weight and tried to stretch out occasionally. As they went, she switched which hand was on the steering wheel more and more often.

Sylvia pulled an ear bud out of her ear and tucked it into the strap of her bra. "My turn to drive."

"I'm good to go a little longer," Crystal replied.

No one had said that Sylvia couldn't drive. Sylvia was technically capable. She did drive. Crystal just didn't like the thought of it. Turning the wheel with one hand was tricky on harder angles and in parking lots. If Crystal was this sore from a handful of hours, she didn't want to put that much strain on Sylvia.

Sylvia was slouched down in her seat with her feet up on the dashboard. "It's been, like, three hours. You're tired."

There were little dots on the windshield from where her toes pressed against the glass. She left the ear bud far-thest from Crystal in her ear, tapped her fingers to a beat, and bobbed her head.

"It's not much farther. How about I drive there and then you can drive home?" Crystal suggested.

She looked straight ahead. She wasn't going to let

Sylvia drive home, but she had the whole trip to think of an excuse for why not. Sylvia placed a hand on Crystal's knee. Crystal jumped a little, but still didn't look her in the eyes. Sylvia could read her. She'd know.

Sylvia sat up. "Yea?"

The scenery around them was starting to look rural. The roads were twisting around mountains instead of cutting through them. There were farms instead of houses. Everything was farther apart.

"Thirsty?" Sylvia asked.

Crystal shook her head no, but Sylvia was already rooting around in the bag half of the junk in the car. Her bad hand was pinned beneath her while she looked. She had difficulty sorting through things one-handed. The side of her body pressed against Crystal's shoulder. It knocked one of her hands off of the wheel. She compensated without a sound.

"I love you," Crystal said.

Sylvia was in the back of the car up to the waist. Her butt and legs were close to Crystal's face. Sylvia didn't hear her. She was rummaging with both hands now, but her bad arm wasn't as helpful. Crystal glanced over at her butt and smiled. Sylvia's hips might have been wide, but her butt was comparatively small. Crystal grasped Sylvia's thigh to steady her. The car shifted toward the shoulder, but it wasn't far enough to be dangerous. Sylvia returned to her position in seat. She opened a bottle of soda and handed it to Crystal.

"I love you," Sylvia said.

Crystal held the bottle to her lips, but didn't actually drink any. She set it in the console between them.

"Thanks for driving," Sylvia added.

"I like to drive," Crystal said.

Sylvia took a sip of the drink. Crystal didn't *not* like to drive, so the statement was mostly true. She took the bottle and put it to her lips. The rim tasted like Sylvia's lips. She didn't drink.

"What do you want to do when we get there?" Sylvia stretched while she asked. Her right arm bumped the roof of the car. The left arm only came up about half that distance.

Crystal beamed. "I thought I'd make something for dinner. I brought tons of food." Even the tone of her voice was bright. She was an excellent cook.

It had never been appropriate for her to be so lavish with their meals. Now, she felt like she could spread her wings and show Sylvia what a good homemaker she would be.

"Oh!" Sylvia perked up. "How about pizza tonight? It's the perfect movie food," Sylvia suggested.

Crystal caved in on herself. Sylvia watched her shoulders creep inward. She hunched.

Sylvia hated that hunch. It was so defeated. Her head tilted down enough that she had to move her gaze to see the road. She felt the cord behind her eyes strain.

"We could stop and get some," Crystal offered.

A TURBULENT AFFAIR   99

Sylvia took a sip from the bottle. It crackled under her grip.

"Or maybe something a little more fancy. I mean you are in charge of the food. We already decided," Sylvia reminded her, poking Crystal in the shoulder.

Crystal took another fake sip and offered an unnatural swallowing sound. "If you are in the mood for pizza, let's just stop and get one." She was disappointed, until she reminded herself that the trip was about making Sylvia happy. Giving Sylvia what she really wanted was the best way to show how much she loved her.

"Naw, we can have pizza any time. This is a special trip," Sylvia said. She took the drink back and sipped at it. "I'll drink it all if you aren't careful."

Crystal laughed. That was the plan. She wasn't very thirsty and soda was dehydrating.

Chapter 11

THE CABIN

It was evening before they arrived at the cabin. It took about an hour to get everything inside. Crystal took a few extra minutes to organize the food into the cabinets. The frozen and refrigerated food had begun to thaw. Everything else was moist from melting ice in the cooler.

Sylvia jumped onto the bed. Her legs and arms were vertical lines on the spread. Crystal finished her chores and entered the room. Without speaking, she cuddled against the side of Sylvia's body. Sylvia let her eyes meander around the room. She avoided looking at Crystal. Her heart was beating quickly. There was no television in the bedroom. It wasn't that sort of bedroom.

Crystal crawled over Sylvia to the edge of the bed and set her phone down. There was a nightstand on either side of the bed. Sylvia's was closer, but not much closer. It would have been just as easy to place it on her own side.

At first, Sylvia remained tense, but she separated her thighs a little. Crystal lay in-between the gap her legs made. She rested her chin near Sylvia's belly button, lifting herself up so it wouldn't put pressure on Sylvia's belly.

"What do you want to do now?" she asked.

Sylvia pressed her lips together and moved them back and forth. Crystal nuzzled her. She slowly flipped up the edge of Sylvia's shirt and kissed her exposed belly.

"I—uh—" Sylvia stammered.

The closer they had gotten to the cabin, the more uneasy Sylvia had felt. She wasn't sure if she could trust herself alone with Crystal like this. It was worse that the area was isolated. The cabins on this end were far apart. Beyond the ring of housing there were tent campers. Sylvia reminded herself that romantic getaways were supposed to be secluded.

Her voice was gruff. It had that I-haven't-spoken-in-several-hours roughness around it. She cleared her throat. It forced her body to bob and broke the contact of Crystal's kiss. Crystal looked up at her. Sylvia didn't look like she was having fun. She looked lost in thought.

"Are you too hot? I can turn the fan on," Crystal offered.

Sylvia wiped her forehead. Her face was reddening. She was sweating a bit without realizing it. She wiped her right palm on the sheet. The arm wrapped in gauze didn't bother to move at all. "Not too hot." She swallowed roughly. It went down wrong. She coughed violently.

Crystal immediately sat up to take weight off of her. Sylvia curled her body and coughed. She held her good hand in a thumbs up. Between coughs she tried to talk. "Swallowed. Crooked."

"It's okay. Cough it out. I hate that," Crystal said.

She moved to sit behind Sylvia.

Sylvia stopped coughing. She took a few impossibly deep breaths to clear her airways. "Kkmm-kkmm." She cleared her throat again. "Sorry about that."

Crystal hugged Sylvia from behind. "Are you okay now? Can I get you anything?"

"A drink, maybe?" Sylvia asked.

It would be nice to have a little space. Crystal left the room. Sylvia straightened her hair. She stuck the thumb of her left hand in her mouth sideways, lightly pressing her teeth against it.

She looked down at the bed. It was a beautiful spread. The sheets were something between barn red and burnt orange. The comforter was brown and gold. Fall colors—no doubt staged for relaxation. They had driven all day.

It was dark. She was inexplicably tired, even though they hadn't really done anything except sit in the car.

"Doesn't that hurt?" Crystal asked.

She stood in the doorway with two wine glasses. There was a bottle tucked under her arm. Sylvia let her hand drop. There were small teeth indentations in her thumb. *That was fast,* she noted mentally.

Crystal sat on the bed and placed the two glasses in-between them. She dislodged a corkscrew from her pocket and let out a frustrated puff of air. It was immediately obvious that she wasn't strong enough to open the bottle.

"If I hold the bottle, do you think you can do it?" she asked.

Sylvia stared at the corkscrew. It was sharp enough. She wasn't sure she had enough strength to do it one-handed. Crystal positioned her hands around the top and sides of the bottle. Sylvia held the corkscrew tightly. If she wasn't accurate, then it would have scraped across the topmost part of Crystal's fingers. Sylvia visualized her creamy skin caught under the corkscrew. It was horrible.

She pulled her eyebrows together. The skin on her jaw was taught. The bite marks in her thumb were throbbing, though she hardly felt it. Crystal smiled the same goofy smile she always gave Sylvia. Nothing had changed between them.

"I can get it. Just make sure to brace it," Sylvia ordered.

Crystal held the bottle between her knees with her hands on top. Sylvia placed her withered hand over Crystal's to protect it. Her fingers loosely cradled Crystal's tiny hand. They opened the bottle of wine.

"Are you okay? Is something wrong?" Crystal asked.

"Everything is fine," Sylvia assured her.

She leaned against her bad arm. The pain brought clarity to her thoughts. She'd told herself she didn't want to hurt Crystal. It was true. However, she was still afraid she would.

Crystal poured the wine. She sipped hers. "Fine" wasn't an encouraging answer. When Sylvia said fine it translated to something negative. She wasn't fine. Sylvia took a few big gulps of wine and smiled at her.

"Do you like it here?" Crystal asked.

"Yea. Of course. It's good. I like it a lot," Sylvia answered.

Crystal balanced the bottle on the floor. "What do you like about it?" She was being genuine. She wanted to start conversation and keep the mood light. She wondered if Sylvia was nervous about being alone with her.

Sylvia wanted to contribute. She wanted to tell Crystal that she couldn't focus. She felt far away because she was feeling the fear that Crystal should have felt. Sylvia wanted to tell Crystal that this wasn't a sex trip. She wasn't ready.

Instead, she made random noises. Nothing coherent came out of her lips.

"If you don't like it, you can say that. I won't be up-set or anything," Crystal lied.

She studied the look on Sylvia's face. The corkscrew lay discarded on the bed.

"It's such a nice night. Do you want to go for a walk?" Sylvia asked.

"It's getting late," Crystal replied.

It was a passive-aggressive thing to say. She knew it was. Crystal didn't like the thought of walking in the dark. However, she had asked Sylvia what she wanted to do. If that's what she picked, Crystal couldn't refuse. She crossed to a window and looked out. Sylvia took advantage of her distraction to drink the rest of her glass of wine.

"Okay," Crystal conceded. She stretched her arms above her head. "Let's go for a walk. The fresh air will be nice after being cooped up in the car for so long."

Chapter 12

THE WALK

Crystal hovered close to Sylvia's side. She wrapped her arm around Sylvia's waist while they walked. Every so often their feet stumbled against each other from the proximity. Crystal squeezed Sylvia. Something about the woods at night made her jumpy. Her nervousness gave Sylvia a little more confidence. Her weakness made Sylvia feel gallant. While they were out walking, it felt like the good old days.

They walked and talked about nothing in particular. Crystal's eyes darted around the narrow paths. She had trouble focusing on Sylvia's words.

Eventually, the conversation fell away. Sylvia was

careful not to stray too far from the cabin. Crystal leaned into Sylvia. Her hair blended into the darkness of the air around them. She was standing tall. Her legs were long and lean. Crystal easily could have tripped her, if she wasn't careful. Sylvia wouldn't be able to use her left arm to brace herself if she fell. It was too sluggish to re-act that quickly.

"What was that sound?" Crystal asked.

She stopped in her tracks. The loss of momentum jerked Sylvia forward. They stopped abruptly. Crystal was frozen in place. Her knees were shaking. It wasn't pitch black, but the lighting was dim and scattered. Sylvia pressed herself close to Crystal. She breathed as evenly as possible.

Crystal's eyes were big and round. They were full of fear. Sylvia smiled at her childishness.

"Animals, trees, wind, us, probably other campers. It's the woods at night, and we're city people. It's sup-posed to sound a little strange. It doesn't bother me as much as silence would. Silence in the woods means dan-ger," Sylvia commented.

She wrapped her right arm around Crystal's waist. The two took a few shaky steps, but being so interlaced was difficult for Sylvia.

"Do you want to go back?" Crystal whimpered.

Moonlit night walks were supposed to be romantic. She was too anxious to make it work. She bit the nails on her right hand. There wasn't much nail left to start with.

Her index and middle finger were down to the quick before Sylvia responded. "I kind of like it."

Sylvia glanced up at the sky. Glittering stars shone down on them. The tops of the trees caught light from the moon. The reflection of that light settled into Crystal's eyes. It was beautiful. Crystal opened her mouth to speak, but Sylvia kissed her before she could. It wasn't an overly puckered kiss. This kiss was tight and strong. Something about it was almost compulsive. Sylvia let the edge of her guard down. It was the kind of kiss she gave Crystal when their love overwhelmed her sensibilities.

Crystal's jaw popped. When Sylvia pulled away, Crystal's teeth smashed together. "So, you don't want to go back?" she asked.

Sylvia laughed at her. "You want be in a cabin, in the middle of nowhere with *me*, but you are afraid to walk in the woods?" She snorted then laughed a second time.

Crystal gripped the back of Sylvia's T-shirt. "I'm not afraid."

"You might be the most adorable person I've ever met," Sylvia teased.

She meant it as a compliment. Crystal took it as an insult. Adrenaline fueled her anger. She frowned. Angry breaths strained the buttons on her blouse. Sylvia could see the faint outline of her bra underneath.

"You'd rather get eaten by bears than be alone with *me*, so who is afraid?" Crystal shot back.

The pitch of her words rose in the center. Sylvia

tightened her grip. The tenderness in their embrace shifted to something colder.

"It's not that," Sylvia said.

She detached herself from Crystal and walked a step forward. Crystal walked alone without losing her composure. She was meek. She was soft. Sylvia knew it would frighten her. That was the point. *Who was afraid? Tell me, who should be afraid?* Crystal followed as closely to Sylvia's heels as possible without touching her. She didn't have permission to touch her.

Sylvia breathed in the night air and held it. "This is creepy. It's scary. I like that. It makes me feel more like myself."

"What can I do?" Crystal asked.

A noise startled both of them. Crystal jumped forward, practically on top of Sylvia. Sylvia kept Crystal's body behind her, so that she stood between Crystal and the noise. "It's okay. I've got you," she whispered.

"Don't let go, Sylvie," Crystal begged. She buried her face in Sylvia's back. The cotton of her T-shirt was rough against Crystal's skin. Wisps of Sylvia's hair blew back into Crystal's face. "Don't ever, ever let go of me."

"What?"

Sylvia wanted to look back. She wanted to see Crystal's face. She surveyed the woods for signs of danger. Low hanging branches were swaying gently in the breeze. They made a whooshing sound when they touched. Despite the season, the ground was covered in brush. Leaves, twigs, and dust rolled lazily on the forest floor. As to signs of danger, there were none.

"I'll disappear. Without you, I'll just fade away. I don't exist," Crystal whimpered.

She kissed Sylvia hard on the shoulder blade. Sylvia turned. She wrapped both arms around Crystal and forced her injured hand to close around Crystal's waist. The fabric of Crystals button-up was blended wool. It was warm from Crystal's skin. Sylvia smiled. She remembered thinking something remarkably similar once.

"It's just other campers, there is no reason to be so jumpy," she said.

"Other campers?" Crystal asked. She squinted into the darkness. Her eyes weren't as sharp as Sylvia's.

"They are probably out here walking like we are, or they wondered off for firewood or to pee in the woods or something," Sylvia said. She touched Crystal's cheek. It was cold. The heat of her body pooled in the middle. Sylvia wished she had a jacket to wrap around her. "I'm right here, Crys. Right here with you. Let's go back now. The cabin is this way. We haven't gone far."

Sylvia tried to turn. Crystal didn't move. Her feet were planted firmly on the ground. Sylvia loosened her grip. She wasn't strong enough to move her by force. Sylvia and Crystal locked eyes. Their breaths intermingled. Crystal didn't look like Sylvia had expected. Suddenly, her face was full of resolve.

"Are they close?" Crystal asked.

Sylvia was bewildered. Crystal clasped her hands to-gether in front of her. It stopped them from shaking.

"I don't—why?" Sylvia listened.

The noise of bugs and animals was quieting. They were pretty close, whoever it was. They were stumbling, loud, and possibly drunk.

"It's dangerous to wander around the woods at night," Crystal stated.

A crooked smile spread across her face. She had ag-onized over how their relationship would work—if it could work at all. They couldn't be without each other. As it was, they couldn't be with each other, either. They didn't know how. Something had to bend. Crystal won-dered if she could use this situation to prove her point.

Sylvia's heart raced. Her arm felt heavy. Her body began to tingle. It was a shiver of anticipation she knew well. It wasn't clouded with fear. The emotion was intox-icating. "If you are suggesting what I think you are sug-gesting, then don't. That isn't what I am."

Her pupils dilated. It was exciting to fantasize about Crystal, but the numbness in her arm reminded her how futile the fantasy was. She couldn't do it. That's why they could be together. She couldn't cross that line, even if she found the physical strength. It would be the end of them. Sylvia remembered the way Crystal looked at her the night she told her that she liked to hurt people. She had to be normal now.

"I could do it. You could show me," Crystal said.

Sylvia's eyes widened at the suggestion. For the smallest instant, she looked horrified.

Lots of couples had weird quirks in the bedroom. Sylvia's cheeks went red. The blush spread across her face until it touched her ears. She shook her head violently. Crystal thought she was saying no. In reality, Sylvia was trying to push away thoughts that were creeping into her mind. Her body betrayed her. She pressed more tightly against Crystal. The firmness of her passion made Crystal gasp. Sylvia saw her with hungry eyes. It reminded her of their first kiss. This was Sylvia in her truest form, the part of her she tried to hide from the rest of the world. Crystal wanted to understand her. She wanted to be a part of her.

This is what it's supposed to be like, Crystal thought. *It feels so good.* She drank in Sylvia's scent. Crystal wanted this. She wanted them to be like this. She wanted the touching, kissing, and sex, to be this easy. Not just once, or when Sylvia lost control. She wanted it to be like this all the time. If she could find a way to tear down that wall and show Sylvia she could handle it, then she could make that dream a reality.

"No," Sylvia said.

Her words were unconvincing. Crystal was too sweet. She was fragile. Something like this would break her. It was risky. It wasn't worth it. Rationally, Sylvia knew it wasn't. Crystal licked the side of her face. Sylvia shivered. Her heart jumped into her throat.

"You don't understand, but it's my fault. You always try to, and I never let you. It's about the intimacy, the trust, the vulnerability. I'd never hurt a stranger for my own gratification, no one should ever put their own appetites above the will of another person," Sylvia explained.

Crystal was using her own desires against her, manipulating her. She reached into her back pocket and pulled out the corkscrew. She held it out to Sylvia. "I *do* understand. That's the reason I know it's not as dangerous as you keep saying it is, but we have to be able to talk about it. I saw you staring at this thing. I'm not stupid. You aren't putting your desires above mine, I want you to," Crystal said.

Sylvia took the corkscrew from Crystal and tossed it to the ground. She felt sick. She was disgusted with herself for being tempted so easily.

"Let me do *something* for you," Crystal begged. "Give me a chance."

"I hurt Jason. He could barely talk when he left my place. I've broken my boyfriends' noses, ribs, and fingers. I told you that night. Things get carried away if you let them. Even if you both want it at the time, there can still be unexpected side effects. I can't risk doing something like that to you," Sylvia said.

She looked at Crystal. She was beautiful. She was clever. She was sweet. Sylvia loved her. She felt suddenly overwhelmed by her love. It soaked into her skin like sunlight and filled every part of her body.

Crystal sighed. "Your arm is weak. Yes, I'm a woman, and I am probably more fragile than Jason, but you aren't strong enough to seriously hurt me. Maybe someday you will have to be careful, but not right now. I want to do this. I want you to want me the way I want you. Do you, want me?" Crystal asked.

"He left, Crys. They all leave. People talk. There's too much pressure to be normal. Jason wouldn't even look me in the eyes when he broke up with me," Sylvia responded.

Crystal wondered if she had made a mistake by pushing so hard. It was embarrassing. Sex games. Sex. All couples had to find a way to be intimate. Sylvia tried to pull away.

Crystal stopped her. "You aren't really afraid of hurting me, are you? You keep dancing around it. You say it's not safe, or that you don't trust yourself, but I just proved that you'd never hurt someone who didn't want it. You'd stop if your partner asked you to. *That's* what you told me. I admit, when you first said it I was scared. I'm still a little scared, but I trust you not to go too far. That's not what this is about, it is? Sylvia, do you trust me not to leave?"

"You did leave. When I told you, you looked at me like I was awful. I thought, if you couldn't accept it, no one could. If I couldn't make it work with you, then I couldn't make it work with anyone. I can't be myself," Sylvia whispered.

The voices in the distance faded away. The two girls held each other in the quiet, night air.

"I came back. I got overwhelmed, and I'm sorry. That's who *I* am. I'm anxious and awkward. We have to be able to disagree, to argue, to talk like we used to. You don't love me any less because I'm jittery, and I don't love you any less because you're aggressive. I told you that I don't want a watered down version of you," Crystal exclaimed.

She took Sylvia's uninjured hand and brought it up to the side of her head so that their fingers combed through the hair above her ear. Crystal squeezed her hand around Sylvia's. Then, she moved their hands so her head was forced to move in the same direction. A gentle heartbeat of pain pulsed into the side of her scalp. It hurt, but the sensation wasn't intense enough to be unbearable.

"Go ahead," Crystal ordered, reassuring her.

Sylvia lightly touched Crystal's uncovered ear with the tip of her nose. She rubbed her cheek along the side of Crystal's exposed neck. The skin was soft. Sheen from her paleness caught what little light there was underneath the canopy of trees. When Sylvia bit the skin on her neck, Crystal's body tensed. Instinct told her to pull away, but she tilted her hips toward Sylvia's. It wouldn't sting as sharply if she relaxed her muscles.

The women's breaths pooled in the middle when Sylvia released her. They scanned each other's eyes for signs of distress. Crystal nodded. A cool breeze passed over them. Sylvia stepped forward. Her weight moved Crystal backward until she slammed into a tree on the edge of the path.

"Tell me if you don't like it," Sylvia ordered.

"What do I say?"

"Anything. Just something that you wouldn't normally say," Sylvia suggested.

Sharp pieces of bark grated against Crystal's back. Sylvia shifted her weight from foot to foot. She licked Crystal's lips from the bottom of her chin to the tip of her nose. Crystal's heart pounded. Her mind went blank. Sylvia's wide, round eyes waited for her to respond.

"Red light?" Crystal asked. She expected Sylvia to laugh. It was the only thing she could think of. "Green means go. Red means stop." She blushed.

It would have been better if she had said something sexier. The phrase red light was too much like the game you played as children. Of course, thinking of it that way did make her feel more in control.

"Yes. Red light," Sylvia confirmed.

Crystal felt the crushing pressure of Sylvia's body against hers. She puffed in a few shallow breaths since her lungs couldn't fully expand. Sylvia bit the edge of her jaw hard enough that a crescent row of teeth marks marred the skin. Crystal tried to shift to a more stable position, but only succeeded in throwing them both off balance. They slipped off the side of the tree and fell backward.

They hit the ground with a thud that took the wind out of them both. Their legs tangled up. Sylvia curled her injured arm against her so it would be protected from the brunt of the fall. She immediately gripped the side of Crystal's collar and pulled it hard to the side. The seam in the neck snapped and popped as the threads stretched.

Crystal blinked. A red line formed where the fabric pulled against her skin. *What should I do? Is it okay to enjoy this?* She wrapped her arms around Sylvia's neck and pulled her down. The force of the embrace brought their faces close enough to kiss. The tips of their tongues flipped over each other. Crystal cupped a hand around the side of Sylvia's breast. The other hand groped over the curve of her butt.

"Mm, Sylvia."

Crystal shifted her weight sideways to signal that she wanted to switch positions. The two girls rolled deeper off of the path into the edge of the woods. For a moment, they both struggled to be on top. Sharp sticks and rocks crackled underneath them. Burrs stuck to their clothes and leaves jumbled Crystal's hair. Sylvia moved Crystal with enough force to strike parts of her body into the ground and bruise the skin stretched over her wrists and ankles. The firmness of the earth chaffed her spine.

Sylvia smiled when she won the top position. She moved Crystal's hands back to her breasts so that she would understand that she had permission to participate as much or as little as she wanted. Sylvia's fingernails roamed underneath Crystal's clothes and marked uneven lines in the skin. She pinched and twisted the tight skin around her ribcage. Crystal inhaled sharply. Sylvia paused to give Crystal the chance to speak.

Crystal let her arms fall limp above her head, leaving her body open to Sylvia's ravaging. She moved her fingertips over the grass and dirt underneath them. Sylvia kissed the spot on her belly where her shirt lifted away. Crystal squeaked when her hand landed on a thorny plant. The area around them was too shaded to see it well. The skin separated slightly in a few jagged scratches. Sylvia noticed. She pulled a sprig off of the plant and passed it over the exposed skin on Crystal's belly.

Even so, Sylvia cradled Crystal with fondness. To anyone looking on, it might have looked like they were beating the hell out of each other. In reality, there was care and restraint in Sylvia's actions, even when she bit, scratched, and tugged on the skin. She pressed, smacked, and bent Crystal's limbs, but she did so with an undertone of affection.

Crystal's hand slid between Sylvia's thighs. Sylvia froze the instant Crystal's fingertips brushed against the zipper on her pants. Her breath heaved quietly into the night air. In the stillness, Crystal noticed the bugs' faraway chirping, and the way the trees rustled in the wind above them. The world came back into focus.

"Red light?" Crystal asked, unsure.

"N—no," Sylvia answered.

Chapter 13

DAY'S END

Crystal leaned her body against the back of the bathroom door. Behind her, the faucet poured steaming water into the tub. Bubbles formed around the edges of the water. The scent of lavender wafted into the air. Music drifted through the closed door. She checked the temperature of the water with her hand. It was scalding. Dirt billowed out from her hand, into the water. She stared into the mirror above the sink. Her skin was pale. It looked like porcelain, like alabaster. The white of her flesh contrasted smudges of soil around her cheekbones. It made them look more prominent. Her lips were swollen. For the first time, *she* was a beautiful mess.

Crystal admired her reflection. Steam poured into the room. The heat kept the sweat and mud on her body from drying. Her fingertips throbbed. Dirt crusted so thickly under her nails that she could feel them pulling away from the nail bed.

She walked robotically toward the sink. Her mind was far away. She grabbed her toothbrush and began to brush her teeth. Dryness in her mouth made her teeth stick to her lip. Her throat was parched. She rinsed and spit with the cup her toothbrush had been sitting in. She filled the cup and drank. She gulped down every drop without breathing, until her lungs begged for air. She filled the cup again and drank again. Crystal set the toothbrush down on the sink. Sylvia's toothbrush was laying on the counter.

When Crystal laid her brush down, one toothbrush was facing to the right, and the other was facing to the left. She studied them. After a few seconds, she flipped her toothbrush over and nudged it so that the bristles of both toothbrushes were touching. She turned off the faucet before the tub got too full to fit both of them.

She unhooked her bra with one hand and slipped the straps down off of her arms without removing her shirt. The button on her pants pressed into the skin of her belly. Crystal freed her legs from the pants. Before leaving the room, she folded them and placed them in a corner.

Sylvia perched on the edge of the bed, waiting for her.

Crystal felt simultaneously exhausted and hungry. "Bath's ready," she said. She sucked in a deep breath and smiled.

"Never mind that, come here." Sylvia's command was quiet.

Crystal was afraid for a moment that she had misheard. She pressed her bare legs against each other. They were smooth and silky. Normally pale, her skin was blotchy from the exercise of romping through the woods. Crystal's smile grew wider. She flattened down a bird's nest of tangles in her hair.

"Come here," Sylvia ordered again.

Her head dipped lower when she spoke. Crystal felt Sylvia's eyes wandering over her. She glided over to the bed and sat next to where Sylvia was sitting. Sylvia crawled on top of her. Her weight pressed Crystal slowly into a prone position. Sylvia laid her head on Crystal's chest and listened to the rapid, raging sound of her heart beating. Her breasts were soft. Before Sylvia and Crystal started dating, Sylvia had no idea how soft breasts were. She never gave her own breasts a second thought. They were so small. She nuzzled the side of Crystal's breasts with her nose. It quickened the pace of Crystal's heartbeat.

Sylvia unbuttoned the topmost of Crystal's buttons. The skin-on-skin contact made Crystal gasp. Her hand flew to the buttons to help, but Sylvia lightly pressed her injured hand into Crystal's palm. Sylvia couldn't bear any weight on the arm, but she used it as a prop to guide Crystal's actions.

"You gave me what I wanted. I can be gentle for you. I can move softly. Relax, love," Sylvia instructed.

Crystal tried to relax. She rested her arms in smooth lines above her head. Sylvia unbuttoned Crystal's shirt with her free hand. The position shifted her weight onto her knees. If it was challenging, she gave no sign of it. She kissed Crystal's belly.

"I love you so much," Crystal said.

She said it often, but it never diluted her conviction. She thought about all the times she wanted to say it and couldn't. Her muscles ached. She wanted this. She had spent years wanting this. Now that they were here, Crystal was suddenly afraid of doing something wrong.

Sylvia's mouth moved lower on her body. Stiff muscles softened under Sylvia's touch. Crystal wasn't sure what she should be doing. Nervousness left her motionless. Sylvia licked the thin skin above her hip bone. Crystal arched her back. She tried to hold still. Subtle pangs of pleasure coursed through her. It was like a thunderstorm consuming clear skies. The sensations were distant at first. They gathered intensity as they moved across her hips to the inside of her thighs.

"I've never—" Crystal's voice shook.

Her knees were trembling. Sylvia held her body firmly. Crystal gripped a handful of blankets in each hand. Thoughts about what she was supposed to do, or what Sylvia wanted her to do, fell away. Her mind groped for some kind of rational thought. There was a vast expanse of nothingness beyond the feeling of Sylvia's touch. Crystal's body trembled. The sensation was overwhelming.

"And I love you," Sylvia said, pulling away from her.

She raised her head far enough to look at Crystal. Crystal's eyes were closed. She crossed her arms over her chest. The nubs of her fingernails on each hand gripped onto the tops of her shoulders.

"I—I—I—" Crystal stammered.

Her hands slid up her neck and covered her face. She tried to steady her breathing into her palms, like using a paper bag to keep from hyperventilating.

Sylvia moved to lay beside her. She pinned her injured arm underneath her and used her good arm to pull Crystal into the cloth of her shirt. Tears spilled out of Crystal's eyes. She kept her face covered. Sylvia held her closer. The edge of Sylvia's knee slid between Crystal's legs. Crystal's wrapped herself around Sylvia and dug her fingernails into Sylvia's back. Sylvia touched their foreheads together. Crystal's pupils dominated her eyes. Through the tears, Sylvia could barely see any color circling them.

"It's so much, so perfect," Crystal whispered when she found her voice again.

She tried to stop crying, but couldn't. She wasn't

sure what she thought it would be like. There was no way to describe it. Crystal wanted the moment to last forever. She clung to Sylvia.

A smile crept across Sylvia's lips. Crystal kissed her. For an instant, Sylvia pulled against the kiss. Her lips and chin were sticky with moisture. The feeling of Sylvia's tongue in her mouth reminded Crystal's body how sensitive it was. She broke the kiss prematurely with a low pitched moan.

"Shh," Sylvia whispered. Her tone was somewhere between the firmness of reassurance and the softness of comforting. "Should we make that bath a cool shower instead?" she teased.

Crystal giggled. Her tears subsided. She moved her shaky legs tentatively. "You know, I don't think that I can stand up," she admitted.

She imagined a deer taking its first bowed steps on newborn legs. It would ruin the moment if her knees caved in and she slid to the floor.

Sylvia grinned at her. "That's okay, Crys," she said. "We are exactly where we need to be."

THE END

About the Author

Sarah Doebereiner is a short story author from central Ohio. She graduated from Wright State University in 2010 with her BA in English. When she isn't writing, Sarah dotes on her two small children. Doebereiner believes that a career in the creative arts is only possible through the support of like-minded people. Macabre themes fascinate her because of their tendency to stay with readers long after the book closes. Her work has been included in anthologies from various small presses.

www.ingramcontent.com/pod-product-compliance
Lightning Source LLC
Chambersburg PA
CBHW060619130626
46555CB00002B/565